THE HONEST ACCOUNTANT

SAM SIMPSON

SPL

First Published in Great Britain 2024 by SPL

ISBN 978-0-9554274-3-5

CHAPTER ONE

Friday 18 April 1997

BLAIR SEEN AS KOHL PUPPET IN TORY AD
LORD SUTCH QUITS POLL TO LOOK AFTER MOTHER
CHIRAC PONDERS SNAP ELECTION TO SAVE EMU

Platt liked having lunch at his desk. No need for painful small talk or lumbering waiters, no need for time wasting. It was more efficient. Besides, it was the only chance he got to read the FT in comfort. Reading it on the tube was just too much hassle. Some folk could wrap themselves around the steel poles in the centre of the carriages whilst juggling newspapers and briefcases, but he couldn't.

Platt read the FT in the same way every day: UK corporates, US corporates, the equity prices. He liked method, procedure and order. He noted that Rio Tinto was up 10p and that his other holdings - ICI, GEC and Marks and Spencer - were flat. Still, he relished the prospect of calculating his capital gains this year. Like most accountants, Platt was risk averse. Investments were always Blue Chip traditional stocks - solid and dependable, unspectacular, never unsafe.

He finished his Ploughman's sandwich, neatly quartered the paper and slotted it into the outside flap of his briefcase, gently and meticulously brushing the crumbs from the boardroom table into his hand and tipping them into the bin. He opened the file at the place he had marked with a post-it before lunch and began to work.

Keith Platt was an auditor's auditor. He liked the perfect symmetry of the balance sheet where everything had its place. Every penny in and every penny out - all had to be accounted for, with nothing missed, nothing left out, no softness, no flexibility: just hard, incontrovertible numbers.

Platt had been with Blake and Lander, one of the so called Big 5 firms, since graduating, and he was fast tracking to partnership. Senior manager next year was realistic, then partner in four, or even three years after that. Partner - that was where the real money was. Platt had heard the starting rate for a junior partner was £200K: not bad for a Yorkshire lad from Goole Comprehensive. He thought of the residents of Humber View Close where his parents lived and quickly calculated that it was unlikely that the combined income of the ten households that made up the cul-de-sac would top even £150K. Thinking of Humber View Close and how he had escaped it always gave Platt a warm glow.

Since arriving in London, he had worked religiously on his accent and successfully softened his Yorkshire vowels, which were now difficult to detect when he talked in general conversation and obliterated entirely if he talked on the phone or to partners. Indeed, after six years of careful study and observation, Platt felt that he could pass for any Surrey or Hampshire Lifer.

The boardroom was on the top floor of Caspian House, which was at No. 2 Connaught Lane. The room was glassed on three sides, with the fourth wall the exposed brick of the building itself. Next door, Platt could see the managing director of Caspian Credit, Jonathan Bridger, reclining at an angle of forty-five degrees in his huge leather chair, feet on desk, bellowing down the phone. He could hear the Scotsman through the glass partition, and he soon guessed that he was talking to his boss.

'For fuck's sake, how can I write more business if you don't give me any bloody money?'

Platt caught the eye of Bridger's secretary, June Paterson, as she turned slightly towards her MD and smiled.

'Ever been on the receiving end of one of Jon's verbal barrages, June?' asked the auditor.

'Never, Keith, you know what he's like with his staff, nice as nine pence, never shouts or bawls, and always says please.'

She turned back to her desk and switched on her lamp. This had the effect of making the glass partition between herself and Platt partially reflective, enabling the auditor to surreptitiously study himself.

He was dressed in the uniform of the City accountant: blue suit with thick chalk stripes, light blue shirt and mauve tie. His cufflinks were silver and his black shoes highly polished. On the boardroom table, he could see the firm's black standard issue pilot bag, with the distinctive B&L logo emblazoned in gold on the front flap. Inside the bag were his tools of trade, the auditors' tools of trade. Six incomplete audit files, business cards, pens, audit paper and the obligatory calculator.

He looked more closely at himself and thought that, despite his thinning brown hair, he was ageing well. At the beginning of his career, he'd often thought that, because of his average height and slight build, he lacked the necessary gravitas to progress in the firm. Since then, though, he had learned to compose himself and walk a little taller than his five foot ten inches belied.

Having decided it had been bright enough after all, June Paterson switched off her lamp, and Platt's reflection disappeared. He was mildly irritated that the secretary had ended his affectionate self-appraisal and he looked at her again. She'd been prickly towards him since he'd arrived at Caspian, despite his best efforts to be accommodating. Perhaps she had detected a hint of insincerity in his attentiveness to her, though Platt was always careful to guard against body language with potential to betray his arrogance.

Platt looked around the third floor. The staff were seated in two large rectangles, the largest of which had its longest side running parallel to the windows at the far end of the room, farthest away from where Platt sat. This rectangle was where the thirty underwriters sat. Day in, day out, they assessed the creditworthiness of Caspian's customers.

The smaller rectangle, which was within earshot of Platt, was where the four customer services officers were. It was their job to deal with borrowers who had missed a payment, and who had realised that, by adding together the charges and penalties that Caspian hid in its loan agreements, they were in fact paying interest at a usurious rate of sixty per cent.

Platt could hear one of the staff, whom he'd interviewed during the audit, talking to a distressed borrower.

'I'm sorry sir, but it states quite clearly in the loan agreement at paragraph 46.5 that a late payment will incur a penalty charge of £40.' Platt could see the man begin to doodle on his A4 pad as the customer no doubt sought to explain why those contractual terms didn't apply to him. 'Yes that's right, sir,' continued the staffer. 'The penalty charge is added onto the loan amount, plus there's the additional interest which we have to levy on the interest which hasn't been paid on time, and the interest on the penalty charge, plus of course the interest which is accruing on the loan itself, that's why you still have £3,760 outstanding.'

Platt felt a brief flicker of sympathy for the customer. Some of the calculations used and the terms employed by Caspian were hard enough for him, a chartered accountant, to understand. He thought about the profile of the customer and others like him who were specifically targeted by Caspian. Typically employed in northern manufacturing with a dependent family and living in rented accommodation, customers would sign up for a loan in October or November, just before Christmas.

These were the sort of loans advertised on pages thirty to forty of the tabloid press, or on the pages of Teletext under enticing banners such as, 'Solve your debt problems in one, call Caspian Credit now!'

Platt knew that, for most customers, Caspian rarely provided a solution to anything. Indeed, the company was renowned in the industry for its ruthless debt collection procedures and liberal use of the bailiffs. Perhaps this was why Caspian's parent, Southern and London Bank, had decided to sell out after 220 years, and might explain why Bridger was arguing so much with his outgoing boss.

The thought of the takeover prompted Platt to turn quickly to his file. If things went wrong post-takeover, angry purchasers always looked more closely at the last set of figures audited under the old regime. Although Caspian was only a small part of Southern and

London, and hardly material, nobody was going to use Platt as a scapegoat. No one was going to thwart his partnership ambitions.

The responsibility for the audit, of course, lay with the audit partner, but Platt had heard what had happened after other Blake and Lander fuck ups. Partners were never sacked because they couldn't be sacked. They were legal partners, and besides, to sack, demote or sideline a partner who had made a mistake would be an admission of negligence. No, it was always the audit manager who got the bullet.

Platt thought of the partner on the Caspian job, Silas Craven, and wondered when he would show up to review the files. Platt had never worked with Craven before, but he knew he had a reputation for being demanding and disloyal.

'Really, Keith, you're not still working on those bloody provisions, I've already told you that once the Reds have been in for six months, unemployment will go through the roof and all the muppets who borrow from us will default.' Platt had been so deep in thought, he hadn't heard Bridger come into the boardroom and stand behind him.

The banker continued, 'then they'll introduce a law which lets defaulters off their debts, just because they've lost their job, or their wife's died, or some other bleedin' heart nonsense, that's it, Blair's Bleedin' Heart Brigade we should call 'em, or even Bleedin' Heart Red Brigade.' Bridger chuckled at his own humour and Platt responded with a forced smile.

Platt decided to defend New Labour. 'That's a typically pessimistic bankers' view. Anyway, they've said they'll stick to the Tories' spending plans for two years, or is it three?'

'Don't you believe a word of it!' replied Bridger, warming to his subject. 'You're too young to remember the misgovernment of the seventies, when Sunny Jim Callaghan and the rest of his clowns couldn't organise a piss up in a brewery. They may call themselves New Labour, but they haven't changed.'

Bridger sidled round from behind Platt to the other side of the boardroom table.

'Change of government or not,' said Platt with a provoking smile, 'a cynic might say that Caspian's provisions enabled you to hit budget plus ten per cent, again, just like you did last year and the previous five years, in fact every year since you took over here. It's almost as if you don't want the boys at Group to set you a higher target, say budget plus twenty per cent.'

'What a creative mind you've got for an auditor,' replied Bridger, in a mock hurt tone. 'Are you accusing me of fiddling the books? You and I both know that the level of provisioning is very judgemental. The previous audit managers from your firm never seemed to have any trouble with it.'

Platt wasn't sure why the last remark made him feel defensive. Was Bridger having a general swipe at auditors or just having a go at Blake and Lander? 'Come off it Jonathan,' he replied firmly. 'Provisions are made and released in line with profits, just so the bottom line can look nice and smooth.'

Bridger roared with laughter. 'You'll never make partner with that sort of comment. The level of provisions *must* be right at Caspian because they're signed off by the auditors.'

Platt realised that he couldn't defend his position and was relieved when Bridger changed tack. The banker continued, 'there's your boss taking home, what, say £400K a year, and for what, signing off the odd audit report. Christ, a monkey could do that, and here's me, 102 staff reporting to me, assets worth £400 million. That's real responsibility! And for what? £70K a year and some worthless share options. I need that bonus.'

Bridger walked towards the door then looked back at Platt. 'Other than the provisions, anything else I should be worried about?'

'Just a bit of detail on that rebate we discussed,' said Platt.

A flicker of concern crossed the banker's face. 'Oh yes,' he said hurriedly. 'I'll have a solution to that for you tomorrow.'

Bridger left the room and Platt observed him as he exited. Platt liked Bridger. He had a ready smile, an inventory of one-liners that most comics could only dream of and the ability to produce a deep, natural-sounding belly laugh even after the weakest of jokes. In short, he was a born salesman and an able executive, who had turned Caspian round from near insolvency during the recession to solid profitability.

Platt knew, though, that Bridger had had enough. Despite the swagger and confidence, he was a man on the way out. Commuting down from his Kelso home on a Monday and returning north of the border on a Friday already qualified him as a part-timer. Caspian had been his personal fiefdom for seven years but now he had done all he could with it.

Platt likened him to an early twentieth-century Ottoman Pasha in a far flung outpost, facing an uncertain future after the overthrow of the Sultans on the Southern and London Board. United and Caledonian had their own finance house, with its own MD, which meant that Bridger was likely to become one of the 'synergies' dreamt up by United's advisors when they made the bid. Platt looked around the top floor. Did Bridger's staff realise that they too had been classified as synergies?

Platt turned back to his file and worked solidly until seven. As it was Friday and his girlfriend Sally was expected at the flat later that night, he decided to treat himself to an early finish.

He looked around the office and realised he was alone. The night lighting had already come on and, apart from the boardroom, the only source of light came from the window of the lift at the far end of the room, which, because the lift was on the top floor, acted as a kind of beacon showing Platt the way home.

He meticulously wrote Monday's 'To Do' list and neatly placed it at the front of the open file, which he then flipped shut and locked in the cupboard in the corner of the room. He put on his jacket and coat and picked up his laptop, which, unusually, fit first time into the correct compartment of his computer case.

He switched off the boardroom lights, instantly enhancing the brightness from the lift. As Platt approached, he was disorientated when the room plunged into darkness. Someone had called the lift from below. There was only one lift, so he pressed the call button and waited.

He was surprised it didn't come immediately. He waited. The button was still illuminated in the call position. There was no sign of the lift coming. It was a Friday, and he wanted to start his weekend.

Frustrated, Platt set off down the stairs. The stairs circled the lift as they descended to the ground floor, and, as he drew near the landing on the second floor, he heard the lift's motor start in response to the request he'd made a few moments before.

Continuing his descent, he reached the first-floor landing at the same time as the lift. He glanced at the small window in the lift door as it sped past. The window on the outer door was parallel with the inner door window for a split second, so Platt only caught a brief glimpse of the man inside.

The man looked directly at Platt and appeared to recognise him. Platt was certain he'd never met the man before. The man's eyes had a dark, callous, lifeless quality to them that he would have remembered. He felt uneasy.

Platt reached the foyer of the building and saw that the security guard, Jim, wasn't there. Platt could smell cigarette smoke and see the half-completed Sun crossword on Jim's desk.

'Hello, Jim,' he said nervously.

Platt heard the lift stop at the third floor.

Jim had a habit of wandering off and had been disciplined by Bridger for deserting his post once too often. Platt stepped out of the building and looked up and down Connaught Lane. To his left he could see the traffic on Buckingham Palace Road, and, to his right, at the far end of the street, past the multi-storey car park, he could see the lights of the Duke of Connaught pub.

Platt jumped as he heard a shuffling noise at his back.

'Didn't mean to frighten you,' said Jim, with a condescending look. 'Call of nature, you know.'

'Has anyone odd gone into the building in the last few minutes?' asked Platt hurriedly.

'Just those Albanian cleaners,' replied Jim. 'They're all bloody odd looking.' Any foreigner was Albanian as far as Jim was concerned.

'I thought there was someone a bit odd in the lift just now,' said Platt, feeling foolish. 'Maybe I was mistaken.'

Jim looked concerned. 'Probably that one with the skinhead. I'll call Len down to watch the desk and I'll pop up to have a look.'

As Platt turned right into the lane and bid Jim good night, he wondered how handy Jim would be against a determined intruder. Obese, sixty plus, and wheezing like a miner, he typified the ex-servicemen gone to seed who topped up their paltry pensions with night shift security work.

Platt chuckled to himself as he thought of Jim's backup, Len, or Limping Len as the girls in Accounts called him, who was just as fat and unfit as Jim, but a little less mobile. The thought of the pair successfully tackling a determined intruder was risible. Jim was probably right, though. Platt was being paranoid.

Platt crossed to the other side of the lane and walked along the road by the side of the multi-storey car park wall. Given that the wall was ten feet high he had little room for manoeuvre when the car hit him from behind. Trapped between the wall and the car, Platt died instantly.

CHAPTER TWO

Saturday 19 April 1997

HOWE ATTACKS DAMAGING TORY AD
GERMANS SEE PUPPET PLOY AS PITIFUL
GOLDSMITH TV DEMAND IS REJECTED BY COURT

Tom Mackay had never been a morning person - he just didn't like getting out of bed. He preferred to ease himself into the day, letting the morning gradually wash over him until he was completely immersed in it. A Saturday morning was no different.

Just for a change he had gone down to The George last night with his flatmates, Atif and Ed, and, just for a change, they drank strong lager, and, just for a change, they waxed lyrical about why they were in The George, by themselves, on another Friday night.

Mackay's hangover was full blown and he felt its kick as he stumbled out of bed and reached for yesterday's clothes. He went down to the kitchen and could smell that Atif had already eaten. Instinctively, Mackay reached for the grill pan.

Sharing a flat with a not very devout Muslim like Atif had its benefits. Atif never really got pissed and could always be relied on to cook himself too much breakfast. Consequently, Mackay gulped down the four fat sausages that lay on the grill pan.

Mackay shaved and showered, then pulled on his beige chinos, blue striped shirt and blue blazer - his election costume.

Given that he was to spend the day canvassing, he thought it prudent to scan over the morning's headlines, so he switched on the small Daewoo TV in the kitchen and looked for the remote control. He found it and brought up the Ceefax news pages, scanning the headlines and observing, 'Poll shows no late swing to government.' No surprise there, he thought.

He left the flat and immediately saw a bus on the other side of the road. On its side was an advert depicting Tony Blair as a ventriloquist's dummy, sitting on Chancellor Kohl's knee. Mackay grunted. Could Central Office get any more infantile?

Mackay was the last canvasser to arrive at the Edwardian terrace in Balfour Street, which was shared by the Barnes and West Putney Conservative Party (ground floor) and the tanning shop (first floor).

He found Annabel sitting alone in the agent's room, one leg on the floor and the other hooked around the edge of the desk, her skirt hitched high up her thigh. Mackay couldn't help but look at her firm legs, long jet-black hair and filled blue polo shirt.

She was aware of his presence but took no action to adjust her position until he rounded the desk, standing four feet in front of her. This prompted her to shift her backside slightly and ground her semi-elevated leg.

'You're here then,' she said sarcastically. 'The rest have already gone. You've got the Cresswell Estate again.'

Mackay tried to hold her gaze, but she was just too attractive. She had very large brown Audrey Hepburn eyes, but her face was fuller and her lips thicker. There was plenty of her to get hold of and snuggle in to, and, as she spun round to get some papers from the far side of the desk, Mackay wondered whether to make a move – she *had* encouraged him before.

He hesitated. Was it worth jeopardising his chances of going any further with her, which was, after all, the whole point of being here in the first place? Months of standing around draughty church halls listening to dreary political speeches and hours spent on rainy doorsteps convincing the constituents of Barnes and West Putney that nice Mr Major should be given one more chance, all wasted because of a clumsy error. Not worth it, he thought, but, despite his mind's rational assessment of the situation, his body was intent on ignoring orders and he reached forward to kiss her.

She half-turned and looked at him warmly before shaking her head, putting the paper she'd reached for into his outstretched hand and smiling. 'Not now,' she said quietly.

Mackay sighed, glancing down at the list, which detailed the alphabetical streets and developments in the Cresswell Estate – Atlee House, Bevan House, Beveridge Close – the list went on. Even in true blue strongholds like Barnes and West Putney, socialists still survived after eighteen years of harassment by the Tories and desertion by New Labour.

Unlike in Kensington and Chelsea (where socialists had disappeared altogether) or in neighbouring Hammersmith and Fulham (where they survived in small pockets), the surviving Reds in Barnes and West Putney were concentrated in one, crumbling, post-war temple to socialism itself, the Cresswell Estate.

'Why do I get all the best wards? Is it that old Roper doesn't like me?' he said in a mock hurt voice.

'Maybe it's because he sees you as the party's best salesman, Tom,' she replied in her creamy fifteen-grand-a-year Cheltenham Ladies' College accent. 'Best equipped for the challenges of Cresswell.' She was too polished to display any sarcasm in her voice or in her expression, but, instead of this having the desired effect of belittling Mackay, it intoxicated him still further.

'It's easy if you truly believe in the prime minister and all that we stand for,' he said, folding the piece of paper in an inspired party activist sort of way. 'It's important that we protect what the government has achieved from left-wing wreckers, Marxists and other such destabilisers.'

She didn't respond, so Mackay blundered on, desperately trying to think what the party's current slogan was. 'It's clear to me that if Blair gets over the threshold at Downing Street it will be a disaster – high taxes for all, Britain isn't working.' He suspected the slogan wasn't quite right, but it rang a bell and his rhetoric seemed to have made an impact on her.

'You're so right, Tom,' she said, looking animated. 'I'm sure that the voters can see this. The polls must be wrong, I know we're right. Mrs Thatcher's legacy can't be put at risk, we must win.'

She got up from the desk and touched his arm. 'Even enemy bastions like Cresswell can be taken, Tom.' She paused, smiled at him, and continued. 'Let's get out there and canvass.'

He looked at her and appreciated her enthusiasm, passion and zeal. For the first time since he'd joined the Barnes and West Putney Conservative Party, he felt fraudulent. She truly had faith in the cause, whereas he didn't really care and simply wanted to bed her. The tantalising thought quickly shelved his brief feelings of guilt, and he set off to sample the delights of the Cresswell Estate.

By late afternoon the dozen canvassers had returned to Balfour Street for Commander Roper's usual pep talk and debrief. Roper was the archetypal Tory party agent: always in blazer and tie, with a thick grey moustache, military bearing and expectations of obedience. He only lacked Victorian sideburns. He was so stereotypical that Mackay suspected that all was not what it seemed with him. Perhaps there was a blemish on his naval record or some financial impropriety, he wasn't sure which.

Mackay noticed Annabel hovering to the right of Roper and tried to catch her eye, but she was too busy feeding the canvass returns into the computer. Mackay hoped she wouldn't notice the beer stain on his return from the Cresswell Estate, which had been picked up in the Duke of Cumberland about an hour earlier.

'Well, people!' began Roper. 'Only ten days to go and still a lot of work to do. Our returns show that it's essential to get our core support out a week on Thursday. Even in a seat like this, there's no room for complacency. What reaction are you getting from the doorsteps? How about the Heston ward, Geoff?'

'Wall to wall blue, Commander,' replied Geoff, 'as solid as a rock. Blair can keep his nose out of Heston.'

This fighting talk initiated a murmur of agreement from the other canvassers and a stifled yawn from Mackay, who switched off until it was his turn to report. Roper always liked to start with the most winnable wards first, and then carry forward his upbeat message and enthusiasm through to hopeless cases, like St Barnabus and the Cresswell Estate.

'Any movement in Cresswell, Tom,' enquired the Commander after about ten minutes.

'Oh yes, definitely a swing to us, Lawrence,' replied Mackay, who was one of the few who called the agent by his Christian name. 'Peter Lilley's pension proposals are going down a storm.'

Mackay didn't feel it was an appropriate forum in which to elaborate on the welcome he'd received from No. 12 Bevan House, where, having introduced himself as the representative of the local Conservative Party candidate, the lady of the house had in turn introduced him to her boyfriend, a man called Headbutt, who in turn had introduced Mackay to his Staffordshire bull terrier, Butch. This last introduction had necessitated Mackay's flight to the Duke of Cumberland and his abandonment of canvassing for the day.

'I always knew pension reform was a vote winner,' beamed Roper. 'I know we are making an impact.' He paused, 'OK, well that about wraps up the debrief. Can I count on you all being at the recreation centre later for Question Time?'

Mackay joined in the subdued laughter and communal head nodding which followed. Roper's attempt at humorously comparing the gathering of the local parliamentary candidates with the BBC's illustrious current affairs programme had clearly hit the mark.

The Heath recreation centre was just off the Lower Richmond Road. As Mackay entered the five-a-side football hall, he was surprised by the large turnout. Quite a few members of the voting public joined the rosette-clad party workers and a sprinkling of local hacks.

The hall was arranged in a similar format to the BBC programme, the only difference being that the 'audience' were not in tiered seating as in the real Question Time. The chairman, complete with Robin Day-style thick brown glasses, was the editor of the local borough gazette, Roger Metcalfe.

Metcalfe first introduced Paul Smith, the Labour Party candidate, who was, according to Commander Roper, 'the usual local government layabout turned trade unionist trouble maker.' Then Metcalfe introduced the bearded Liberal Democrat candidate, described by Commander Roper as, 'a hand-wringing, tree-hugging teacher only lacking a pair of sandals.' Finally, there was the Tory candidate, Silas Craven.

Craven was a partner in Mackay's own firm, Blake and Lander. After years of trawling up and down the Home Counties in search of a safe seat, he had landed on his feet when he'd been proposed by the sitting MP, an ex-partner at Blake and Lander who had stood down after a heart murmur only two months ago.

Mackay enjoyed the debate, which was light-hearted, even jovial, and ranged over the usual topics – the health service, education and defence. Then, an elderly voter asked why the government and the Tory party seemed to be riddled with sleaze.

Mackay looked more closely at Craven as he defended the government. He *was* the archetypal City accountant. He wore a charcoal grey suit with thick, chalky white pin stripes, white shirt, light blue Jermyn Street tie and dark blue braces. His hair was largely greying except at the temples, where it was flecked with silver, giving him a much sought-after distinguished look. He was very closely shaven. His eyes were grey brown in colour and impossible to read. His movements were so measured and smooth that he made the Labour candidate look like a buffoon and the Liberal runner look clumsy. Mackay had to acknowledge that here was a highly polished operator and a brilliant salesman.

'But surely, Mr Craven,' continued the determined elderly lady from the front row, you can't mean that the government has been completely scandal free.'

'There have, of course, been one or two lapses by foolish individuals,' replied Craven, 'but the integrity of the government has remained intact and, as recent polls show, the personal popularity of the prime minister remains extremely high.'

At this point, Chairman Roger Metcalfe, clearly enjoying his role of Grand Inquisitor, half turned to Craven and innocently enquired with a good-natured smile, 'And what about your own integrity, Mr Craven? Any skeletons in your past that may come back to haunt you?'

'What do you mean by that remark?' snapped Craven icily.

Mackay, the other candidates and the audience suddenly became aware that Metcalfe's inoffensive question had released a dose of unpleasantness into the hall, but Metcalfe had missed this. He ploughed on with his nudge nudge wink wink line of questioning. 'Come on, Silas, we all know what you City accountants are like. Which of us wouldn't let our clients cook their books for the enormous fees you lot get? We know the City's just an Old Boys network – don't tell me that you and your firm haven't got your snout in the trough, just like the rest of them.'

Metcalfe had addressed the latter part of his question to the audience, whose anxious faces caused him to turn to look at Craven. He realised that his remarks hadn't been taken in the light-hearted manner in which they had been intended. There was a hush in the football hall.

'Do you stand by those remarks?' said Craven, in a legalistic sort of way.

'I was only joking, of course,' stammered Metcalfe, rapidly reddening.

'Does that mean you don't stand by those slanderous remarks?' probed Craven.

'No. I mean yes,' replied Metcalfe, clearly taken aback by the severity of Craven's tone. Mackay felt sorry for Metcalfe, who had simply got carried away. Craven had unnecessarily humiliated him. The audience sensed this too, as did Craven, who instantly picked up on their sympathy for Metcalfe.

'No harm done then,' said Craven, his treacly smile rotating from Metcalfe to the audience in a slow, 180-degree arc.

The debate was clearly over, and Metcalfe couldn't get out of the football hall quickly enough. He thanked the candidates and audience for coming, announced that the politicians would be available for individual questions for a further half an hour, and, after a quick word with the man with whom he had arrived, he left.

Mackay hung around for a bit, hoping he could persuade Annabel to adjourn to the Cumberland for a drink. He found her locked in conversation with Craven and a voter. This didn't deter Mackay. As he approached, though, he heard the 'Europe' word mentioned. Rather than risk getting roped into a topic he dreaded, he veered off and stood next to Geoff, whom he had earlier seen looking equally as friendless as himself.

Five minutes of Geoff boring him with chat about doorstep canvassing technique was all he could manage, so he suggested that they join Craven, who was now talking solely to Annabel.

Mackay felt uncomfortable as he noticed how she hung on Craven's every word and how irritated she looked when Mackay sidled up to her. 'A polished display, Silas,' said Mackay, with faked enthusiasm.

It was Annabel who answered. 'You handled that awful chairman brilliantly. Poor man went bright red. You would have thought that a professional journalist ought to know better.' She looked at Craven and he acknowledged her support with a flicker of a smile.

'It's important that we remain focused on the real issues,' said Craven earnestly. 'All journalists are sleaze hunters who don't give a damn about the needs and concerns of ordinary people.' Craven sounded so genuine that Mackay half-believed he meant it. Geoff certainly did but, more alarmingly, so did Annabel. Mackay had noticed before and liked how she had a habit of listening with her mouth slightly open. With Craven, though, she seemed to lap up and almost devour his words in a sexual way.

Mackay was glad when Roper joined them but dismayed to discover that Craven had arranged to drop Roper and Annabel off on the other side of the Thames on his way back to Knightsbridge. As Roper lived in Fulham and Annabel lived in Notting Hill, she would be dropped off last and would be alone in the car with Craven. Craven was married and at least fifteen years older than her.

Craven looked at Mackay when they dispersed to collect their bags, then stepped a foot towards him, entering his personal space. He was so close that Mackay could smell his Cologne. He was surprised when Craven touched his arm in a comradely way.

'Sorry to talk shop, Tom,' he began, 'but I have some awful news. Keith Platt was killed in a car accident last night.'

Mackay was stunned. 'Bloody hell!'

Craven continued. 'A hit-and-run driver crushed him against a wall as he was on his way home. He died instantly.' Craven paused. 'Did you know him well?'

'Fairly well. A nice bloke. He was going out with that American secondee, Sally Purcell.'

Craven was expressionless. 'Was he? I didn't know that. She's in your department as well, isn't she?'

'Yes,' replied Mackay. 'Does she know?'

'Probably not. I'll see it's done.' Craven paused, then changed the subject. 'Listen, I know this is bad timing, but Keith was auditing a client of mine, a company called Caspian Credit. It's got a tight reporting deadline and I need a good manager to finish it off. I see from your departmental planner that you're free. Now, as you can imagine, I'm pretty busy with all this and I need someone I can rely on.' Craven hesitated. 'Fancy it?'

Craven looked Mackay directly in the eye. Of course he could compel Mackay to do the job, but that would necessitate a request to

Mackay's departmental partner, which tended to be a political and time-consuming process. Craven continued to eyeball Mackay and somehow managed to engender a sense of comradeship and loyalty in him, which, despite Mackay's endemic cynicism, he found difficult to resist.

'Of course, Silas. Anything I can do to help.'

'Great, thanks Tom. If you could pop into my office first thing on Monday, I'll run you through it.'

Having got what he wanted, Craven's warmth instantly vanished and it was clear that Mackay had been dismissed. Mackay watched him go, with Roper and Annabel bustling around him, he maternal, she possessive. Mackay decided to have a pint in the Duke of Cumberland anyway.

As he stood at the bar waiting to order his drink, the man who Metcalfe had spoken to on his way out of the hall appeared at his side.

'Get you a pint?' said the man.

'OK,' replied Mackay. 'Did you enjoy the debate?'

'Just the usual political crap, though I'll tell you now I won't be voting for your guy.' The man hesitated and waited for Mackay's reaction. Mackay was expressionless so the man continued. 'Still want the pint?'

'Of course. Are you a friend of Metcalfe?'

'A colleague. I work for him.'

The pints arrived and Mackay took a sip. 'At the Gazette?'

'Yes,' replied the journalist.

'Do you expect me to spill the beans on Craven for a single pint of Youngs?' said Mackay with a wry smile.

'No, I've got a £20 note here,' replied the journalist with a grin.

'That's more like it. Let's sit over there,' said Mackay, indicating a booth by the window.

The man was about the same age as Mackay or possibly in his mid-thirties. He was wearing a beige sports jacket, an open-necked shirt and faded blue jeans. He had short close-cropped hair and a worn-out look, which was further emphasised by shadowing around his eyes and thick lines at the corners of his mouth. Mackay noted that he had a south London accent worthy of the terraces of Plough Lane or Stamford Bridge.

'I don't know much,' said Mackay, 'but what I do know is that there's no scandal for you I'm afraid.'

Despite his agreement to do the Caspian audit only a few minutes earlier, Mackay felt no particular sense of loyalty towards Craven. OK, he was a partner at his own firm, but Mackay disliked most of the partners at the firm anyway – Craven was no different. He was just a little oilier than the rest of them and somehow more menacing.

Was Mackay about to breach any confidences? He didn't think he knew any. If this journalist was prepared to supply him with free drink, he was sure he could say nothing slanderous for the time needed to knock back six pints.

'Come on, there must be something,' said the journalist in a light-hearted tone. 'No string of mistresses, drug-taking son, self-asphyxiation with an orange in the mouth, that sort of thing. What about a nice financial scandal? Did Metcalfe touch a nerve earlier when he alluded to all accountants like Craven being bent?'

Mackay turned, looked severely at the journalist and spoke savagely. 'What do you mean by that remark?'

Unlike Metcalfe half an hour earlier, the journalist held his ground, safe in the knowledge that his remark had been made in a private context, rather than in the public arena of a five-a-side football hall.

'What I mean,' continued the journalist firmly, 'is that accountants, auditors, call them what you like, I don't know the difference, are bent. How can they report impartially on a company that pays their fees? How can they be objective when they have audited the same company for seventy or eighty years and the partner is a member of the same club as the chief executive? Do they look after shareholders' interests or simply their own?'

'Do you stand by those remarks?' said Mackay coldly, mimicking Craven.

'Yes,' said the journalist, dismayed that he'd misjudged Mackay and that the conversation was rapidly nearing its end.

'Then go and repeat them in front of those people at the bar. Make your views public. You don't know this but Craven is a partner in the same firm I work for. A slur on him is a slur on me, my colleagues and my profession.'

There was a pause as the journalist took a drink from his pint then picked up his wallet and prepared to leave.

Mackay burst out laughing, 'I'm sorry, I'm only kidding. My impression of Craven was infantile. Get another round in and I'll tell you all about Blake and Lander and Silas Craven, all off the record of course. I'm Tom Mackay.'

'Nick Steadman,' said the man, shaking Mackay's outstretched hand as he got up and headed for the bar.

What a dickhead this guy is, thought Steadman as he ordered the drinks. Another half an hour with him was going to be an ordeal. Metcalfe's instructions to him as he'd left the Heath Centre had, however, been unambiguous. 'I don't care what it takes, I want dirt on that number-crunching arsehole Craven. I want him nailed.'

Metcalfe had been humiliated by Craven, but both the editor and Steadman knew it wasn't the place of the Gazette to go digging about the backgrounds of Tory Party candidates. That work was done by the tabloids. Still, it made a change from the usual cat up a tree type stories that Steadman generally dealt with.

Steadman watched Mackay drain about a third of his pint with his first gulp, tucking his top lip into his bottom lip to clear away the froth that remained.

Mackay sensed that his attempt at humour hadn't been appreciated by Steadman. 'As I said,' he began, 'nothing much to tell about Craven. Been a partner for twenty-odd years, was a fast tracker in his day, just one off the executive board of the firm, but lost out in a power struggle with the current senior partner about three years ago. That ended his rise to the top. Not that he cared much though.'

'Oh, why's that, Tom?'

'Well, during the merger frenzy of the accountancy firms in the eighties, which ended with the so-called Big 6, some partners insisted they get full equity participation in the new firms. Blake and Lander was one of them.'

'What does that mean?' said Steadman.

'New partners and recently promoted partners are either salaried or hold debenture stock in the firm. This means that their payout will be fixed, irrespective of the firm's performance. Craven, on the other hand, is one of the elite few who will not only draw out a fixed sum but will also share in the pot left at the end of the year. In short, he's rich.'

Steadman wasn't interested but he wanted to keep Mackay talking. 'Why don't the new partners split off by themselves, or at least change the rules to vote one of their own in, as senior partner I mean?'

'Three reasons really. The first is greed, in that occasionally one of them is made an equity partner, and, once appointed, the new equity partner quickly becomes reactionary, rather than revolutionary. The second is that they are very risk averse. Training to be an auditor stamps out any entrepreneurial spirit that may have existed at university. The thought of leaving the comfy confines of a Big 6 firm, with all its legal firepower and status, and going it alone, can be scary. The only auditors who have balls are those who set up by themselves and then audit small and medium-sized enterprises, that's real risk, but the partners in my firm would see this as grubby. The final reason is the brand. It's taken years and millions of pounds to develop brands like Blake and Lander. Irrespective of the quality of the service clients receive, the brand can cover up a multitude of sins and give off a veneer of professional respectability, which hides the fact that the firm are just trying to make a buck like any other sharp tradesman.'

Steadman interrupted. 'You seem, bitter Tom. Surely Craven's not that bad.' Steadman was keen to steer Mackay back to Craven.

Mackay, however, was determined to continue his rant. 'I've seen it happen on many occasions. It's easiest with banks or any complex company. Bringing forward income due in three or even five years' time, using provisions to smooth the bottom line so that earnings show even growth, anything to keep the analysts happy. Everyone's a winner in the City gravy train, Nick. The executives get rich because they meet their targets and the accountants get rich on audit fees and lucrative added-on services.'

Mackay paused to drink his pint, before continuing. 'Consultancy is the best wheeze of all. For two million quid you'll get a glossy report in which the consultant tells the chief executive it's raining while pissing on his head. The only losers are the shareholders, who are far too anonymous to worry about. What's a few pence off the value of their individual holdings? Besides,' he went on sarcastically, 'they have the non-executive directors to look after them.'

'I take it you're not intending to progress in your firm then,' said Steadman. 'Won't Craven help you up the ladder? You seemed quite pally with him this evening.'

'No way,' replied Mackay. 'I'm long in my grade already. I'll likely make director in a couple of years then that'll be it, or I'll be farmed out to HR or the training department. They'll hope that I get so bored I'll leave without them paying me to go.'

'I see. And Craven?' pressed Steadman.

'Craven's had enough of the firm now. He wants to get to Westminster, where he can do good and help those less privileged than himself.'

'Do I detect a note of sarcasm, Tom?'

Mackay smiled, then drained his pint and tilted the glass from side to side expectantly.

Steadman got the message and bought another round. 'What about Craven's family?' he said, after he'd pushed Mackay's fresh pint towards him. 'Any tearaway sons, tree-hugging daughters or bigamous marriages?'

'Nothing there for you,' said Mackay. 'No kids as far as I know. His wife Lucinda is an interior designer. I've met her a few times at the office and at the constituency, she's a first-rate snob. That's it, except that he's from up north somewhere. Don't be fooled by the City gent look, he's not Old Money, rather a boy from the Tyne done well.'

'Thanks, Tom,' said Steadman. 'Interesting stuff. As you say, no scandal but plenty for me to put in my pen portraits in the Gazette.'

They continued talking and drinking, until, by closing time, as most boozers do, they had bonded.

CHAPTER THREE

Monday 21 April 1997

BLAIR SNUBBED AS UNIONS PREPARE SHOPPING LIST
SEAMAN AND SHEARER SET TO RETURN FOR ENGLAND
RAMPRAKASH ADDS STEEL TO NATURAL GIFT FOR BATTING

The advantage of living and working in Zone 2 was that Steadman's commute to work was painless, his rented flat only ten minutes from the office. Every morning, as he walked along Lower Richmond Road, he made a point of looking at the gaps in the housing on the north side of the river, through which he could see Putney Bridge tube station and the District Liners standing on the platform.

All stood in silence, preparing for the scrum that would begin when each tube train trundled into the station. Six years ago, Steadman himself had been a District Liner and, even then, it had been a fifty fifty chance of getting a seat. Proper platform management could of course reduce the odds, but now commuters had to go out as far as Southfields if they wanted to avoid the risk of standing. Failure to get a seat meant playing sardines after Fulham, when trains from the Wimbledon, Richmond and Ealing Broadway lines all tried to get onto the same piece of track at the same time - a masterpiece of civil engineering, he thought.

Steadman had toyed with the idea of moving out to Southfields, or even East Putney, where it was cheaper and he stood a better chance of persuading a bank to loan him enough to buy a small flat. Six months ago, he'd even offered on a flat just by the tube but had been gazumped at the last minute. Since then, prices had increased, so he'd resolved to hang on for a month or two and wait for them to fall again, as they surely would.

The offices of the Borough Gazette were on the top floor of an elongated building overlooking the river. The building was utterly incongruous with its turn-of-the-century neighbours and Steadman often wondered how it had got planning permission, even in the seventies.

Metcalfe was already in, and he approached Steadman as soon as he'd dumped his Benjy's coffee on his cluttered desk.

'Get anything out of Craven's sidekick on Saturday?' asked Metcalfe.

'And good morning to you, Roger,' replied Steadman. 'Have a good weekend?'

'Sorry,' said Metcalfe. 'That twat really got under my skin. Good morning.'

'The answer to your question is no, not really. The usual dull but lucrative City career, sounds like his wife is quite demanding, no kids. Just your ordinary rich bloke ready to move up to the next level of Mazlow's hierarchy of needs.'

'Oh, right,' said Metcalfe, with a puzzled look, not really wanting to understand. 'Mazlow – that something you learnt at university?'

'Yeah, I won't bore you with the concept.'

'That's a relief.' The editor paused. 'Nothing else worth looking into?'

Steadman slurped some coffee. 'Doubt it, but I'll do the usual trawling about if you want me to?'

Metcalfe looked disappointed. 'OK, give it a couple of days,' he said, heading to his office.

Steadman's standard public records sweep revealed that Craven's snobbish wife Lucinda was his second wife. There was nothing unusual in that, but from a journalistic angle it was interesting, because a first wife always had a more newsworthy view of her ex-partner than her successor did.

Steadman noted from the marriage certificate that Craven had been married nearly twenty years ago to a Penny Gray, in a place called

Alnmouth, which, after a quick consultation of his Collins road map, he discovered was a small coastal town north of Newcastle.

Then Steadman found Penny Gray's death certificate. There was nothing sinister in that either, except that, after more digging, he uncovered an article in a local newspaper, the Northumberland Journal, which, to Steadman's ever-increasing curiosity, reported that she'd fallen off a cliff. As Steadman hadn't been out of London since Christmas, he decided to test Metcalfe's resolve to 'want dirt on that number-crunching arsehole'.

Steadman was surprised when the editor approved his northern jolly - Craven had clearly annoyed Metcalfe more than he'd thought, - as the travel budget of the Gazette barely stretched to Zone 1 never mind the other end of the country. Steadman was sure the owner of the Gazette wouldn't have seen any journalistic merit in his trip north, but nevertheless he booked a ticket on the first train from King's Cross the following day.

As Steadman was leaving the office that evening, Metcalfe bounded across to him. 'Where there's a first wife there's always sleaze,' he said. 'Sleaze!' He repeated the word, obviously enjoying mouthing it, especially the long zzzzz part, which he seemed to bite into with his front incisors. 'Sleaze,' he said a third time. 'It's endemic in the Tory Party. The only known cure is a good long dose of opposition.'

'That right, Roger?' said Steadman. 'The new lot will be no better. OK, I admit Blair himself is holier than thou, but what about the rest of them? That Robin Cook, bet he's got a string of mistresses. And what about that big Welsh bloke, what's his name, Davies, Ron Davies? Something phoney about him, I'm sure of it.'

'Ye of little faith,' said Metcalfe. 'You just focus on Craven for now, that'll do me.'

'OK, Roger,' said Steadman, pulling on his overcoat. 'I'll see you on Thursday. Hold the front page 'til then.'

'Don't bother coming back without something,' shouted Metcalfe at the disappearing Steadman, 'and Nick?'

'What?' Steadman's face reappeared at the door at the top of the stairs.

'Don't spend more than 200 quid.'

'The train fare's £120,' said Steadman incredulously.

'Things are a bit cheaper oop norf, lad,' replied Metcalfe, in an embarrassingly bad attempt at a Geordie accent. 'Eighty quid will be enuff to gan you through.' But Steadman was already halfway down the stairs, Metcalfe's Gazzaesque tones descending with him.

Steadman liked Metcalfe, who was a reasonable boss and a good teacher. He had rescued Steadman when he'd failed his medical exams and put him on another 'more morally' if not financially rewarding career path. Both men knew that Steadman should have left the Gazette and gone to work for a national years ago. When he was motivated, Steadman had the talent and the ability to deliver fantastic copy, but, as had been the case throughout his life, he was stricken with chronic inertia, which, if not remedied soon, would put an end to his dreams of Fleet Street, or, more realistically now, Wapping.

In truth, swapping the bright lights of London for some miserable former mining town up north didn't appeal to Steadman, but the thought of a night away from his flat and his girlfriend Shannon did. They had been having problems for months now, the problem being that his salary didn't stretch to meals out in the West End or shopping trips to the King's Road every day of the week. According to Shannon, everyone else's did. Her handbags had to be Louis Vuitton, Versace, Chanel, or, at the very least, Mulberry, and her unilateral decision that he should pay all of the rent and that she would make up her share 'in other ways' had worn a bit thin.

Shannon liked everything about London, which he had begun to despise. She was in her mid-twenties, he in his thirties. In his view, therein lay the problem. Any man who is sick of London is sick of life. Steadman wasn't sure who had said this, but he did know that it wasn't true.

London was great if you had a lot of money, you could afford to live centrally, you didn't mind queues and crowds, you could afford not to use public transport, you liked grey instead of green, you preferred fumes to clean air and you had the energy to battle through it all every day and call it life.

Steadman would recommend living in London to anyone. It had to be done, and the T-shirt had to be bought. It was a great experience and had so much to offer for people like Shannon in their twenties, but, for Steadman, like most of his contemporaries, five years was enough, ten was far too many, and fifteen years was just too much.

At dinner at Enotica that night on Putney High Street, he tried to explain to her where Newcastle was and what he was doing there. 'Isn't it near Scotland?' was her one enquiry, after which the conversation turned to her work (at a call centre off the A3) and what she planned to do the following night while he was away. He was surprised at his own lack of paranoia, as she readily confessed that she'd arranged a night out with the girls, which, added to her unusually guarded disclosure as to who the girls were, would normally have aroused his suspicions.

She looked as inviting as ever. Her dark bobbed hair fell repeatedly over her left eye, and she continually arched her back in such a way that her close-fitting white T-shirt rode up above her midriff. Seeing that the French waiter had noticed this, and fuelled with most of the wine, Steadman resolved to get her back to the flat. He took a mental note to savour every second of the experience as something told him it would be the last time.

The next morning, instead of taking the tube to Edgware Road and picking up the Circle Line to complete his journey to King's Cross, Steadman decided to take the overland BR route from Putney to Vauxhall and then use the Victoria Line.

He soon discovered that, while his platform management skills on the tube might still be passable, he had no idea where to stand at Putney BR, and so, despite there being room in some of the forward carriages, he couldn't get on the first train.

The next train, the stopping service, was already twenty minutes late when it came, but it was the points failure at Clapham Junction that really jeopardised his chances of catching the Edinburgh-bound 9.05 from King's Cross.

This is hell, he thought, as he battled down the stairs at Vauxhall, catching a German tourist full in the face with his overnight bag as he accelerated past. Why tourists chose to sightsee through the rush hour, with their enormous rucksacks in one hand and underground maps in the other, was a mystery to him. He couldn't understand how tourists had the audacity to ask distressed commuters the directions to Buckingham Palace or the Tower of London when they could get a cab – there were, after all, plenty of cabbies willing to take them to Buck House or the Tower via Croydon.

Despite the best efforts of London's transport system, Steadman got on the 9.05 with five minutes to spare and headed north.

CHAPTER FOUR

Monday 21 April 1997

Irrespective of the time Mackay got up, he took the same train to work every day. If he got up at 6.30, he ended up running to the station to get the 8.50. If he got up at 8.20, he ran to get the 8.50. Getting the same train was one of the mysteries and certainties of commuting.

If it ran on time, the 8.50 got Mackay in punctually, but it never did run on time and today was no different. Every day, like today, Mackay hid his jacket under his arm and walked past his boss's office in his shirt sleeves, giving the impression that he'd arrived in the office sometime earlier. As he approached this morning, he saw that his boss's door was open and he nervously dreaded a summons from within, but thankfully he was on the phone and Mackay skipped past.

Mackay had the misfortune to share his office with Tony King: the keenest, neatest, straightest and dullest auditor in a department of boring auditors.

'Morning, Tom,' said King. 'Good weekend?'

'Great, Tony,' replied Mackay. 'And you?'

Mackay didn't wait for the reply. He hung his creased jacket on the back of his chair and headed for the coffee machine. By getting coffee before switching on his computer and spreading a few papers over his desk, Mackay risked his poor timekeeping being discovered, but he *had* to have coffee, empty desk or not.

A civilised night with the journalist Steadman after 'Question Time' on Saturday meant that Mackay had no hangover on Sunday. On most Sundays, the combination of a hangover and work the next day provided enough of a deterrent to heading for The George. Yesterday being hangoverless, however, meant that Mackay had been unable to refuse his flatmate's kind offer to buy him a 'quiet one'.

That had been at 4pm yesterday. Twelve hours, 120 quid and thirty units of alcohol later, Mackay had found himself in the West End's Long Island Ice Tea Bar talking to a divorcee called Brenda. The discussion with Brenda had been vitally important at the time (though Mackay now struggled to remember what it was) and had needed prolonging back at his flat, though, once there, the conversation had quickly taken on a sexual nature. The full horror of that dialogue, and the awfulness of its conclusion, had only become apparent to Mackay that morning, when he had woken up next to the veteran Brenda, wrinkles and all. Now he stank of booze and the redness of his eyes was nothing short of demonic. He needed coffee.

Mackay returned to his office, grabbed the nearest file and quickly logged on. The coffee was so revolting that it managed to pierce the fuzziness of his brain, and he began to feel more relaxed as he took on the appearance of someone who was working diligently.

'Feeling a bit rough today?' asked King in a sanctimonious tone from across the room.

'Just a touch of flu I think, Tony,' replied Mackay. 'Must have got it at that outward bound thing the other week. Hope you don't get it.' He could see that King didn't believe him. Why don't you keep your beak out, thought Mackay. Christ, he disliked King, or Wan, as Mackay called him to any sympathetic ear in the department that would listen.

Mackay changed the subject. 'You heard about Keith Platt?'

'What about him?' said King quickly, concern clear in his voice.

The phone rang and Mackay picked it up. It was Craven. 'Tom Mackay?'

'Yes.'

'Silas Craven here. Tom, can you pop up?'

'Sure.'

'See you shortly then.'

Mackay put the phone down and picked up his pen, paper and pass.

'What about Keith Platt?' pressed King.

Mackay was expressionless as he replied. 'Killed on Friday in a hit-and-run on his way home from work.'

'Jesus! Where?'

Mackay stood to go. 'Victoria somewhere. I'm off to see Silas Craven now to pick up the audit. The audit must go on you know.' King was visibly shocked and Mackay realised that his cynicism had, for once, been misplaced. 'Sorry, Tony,' he continued. 'That was a clumsy thing to say.'

'Hmm,' snorted King.

As Mackay left the room and took the lift to the sixth floor, he thought about Platt and King. While he had never got on with either of them, both being as dull as each other, they had of course been kindred spirits and had bonded. Both company men on the partnership track, both happy in auditland. No wonder King had been so shocked. In his calm and measured world of order and stability, death, especially an early death like Platt's, had no place. It just didn't fit in.

Mackay found Craven's office easily. The room reflected not only his revered status within the firm but also his standing as a respected member of the financial community.

Mackay entered and saw a picture of Lucilla - Craven's wife - to the right of the mahogany desk, which sat flush under the window at the far side of the room. The desk itself was inlaid with a green leather writing pad, around which were placed several neat piles of letters, reports and booklets, some of which Craven had marked with different coloured post-its.

Along the wall to the left was an expensive-looking leather sofa, clearly designed to match the writing pad and catch the greens in the Constablesque rural paintings adorning the walls. To the right was a mahogany bookcase filled with audit and accountancy books, which fit snugly between the edge of the desk and Craven's coat stand, where Mackay could see that the beige overcoat and black umbrella were both Burberry.

On the far wall, to the left of the window, where anyone entering the room would see it, Mackay noted Craven's framed certificate showing his admittance to the Institute of Chartered Accountants. The room had a comfortable, expensive, reassuring, and, above all, respectable feel to it – it was all *too* perfect. Mackay wondered whether it actually stood for anything. Was it simply a veneer?

Craven was sitting with his back to Mackay, the visible part of his red braces forming a cross above the chair like a hazard sign. As Craven didn't seem aware of his presence, Mackay cleared his throat. Without acknowledging the signal, Craven continued writing and so Mackay continued to stand.

After about thirty seconds the partner put down his pen and turned slowly in his chair to face the audit manager. Mackay looked away, unable to hold his stare. The warmth and charm of Saturday was gone. Craven looked at him without seeing him. To Craven, Mackay was a nobody.

'Right, Tom,' said the partner, 'Caspian Credit.'

'Much to do on it?' said Mackay, trying to sound keen.

'The audit work is finished, and I think Keith had just about completed his review. He did mention there were one or two loose ends that needed tying up. I was due to go out for my review this week.'

Craven flicked through his standard issue Blake and Lander diary as he spoke, before continuing in the same flat tone. 'I guess we should push that back a week or so now, give you a chance to familiarise yourself with the files and the issues.' Craven paused. 'How's the department reacting to Keith's death?' He added the last sentence as an afterthought, annoyed with himself that he'd forgotten his earlier mental note to ask it first.

'Not many folk know yet,' replied Mackay. 'Any word on catching the driver?'

'No. I spoke to the MD of Caspian about half an hour ago. He said that the police were interviewing staff. Unlikely any of them were still there that late on a Friday. His name's Jonathan Bridger, the MD, I mean. Nice chap, you'll like him.'

'Anything I should know about Caspian?' asked Mackay. 'It's part of Southern and London, isn't it?'

Craven's mind had moved on – this meeting was over. 'Yes, but only the fag end of the retail lending division. The book started going bad during the recession, but Bridger's turned it round. They typically lend £5k to Joe Northerner who loses his job and gets screwed by Caspian on late payment and admin fees. If you add up all their fees their average lending rate is something like fifty per cent. They're not popular with the regulator. Any excuse and the Bank of England will be down on them like a tonne of bricks. It's no wonder Southern's been trying to get rid of them for years.'

Mackay, who was still standing, could see a small passenger jet approaching St Paul's heading for City airport. He could hear the engines despite the reinforced terrorist-proof glass in the window. As it flew over the cathedral it appeared to be speared by the small spire on top of the dome, then it banked left and turned downriver. He had been distracted for only a moment, but he sensed Craven's irritation. 'Sounds like a tidy business,' Mackay said quickly. 'They part of what's being flogged to United?'

'Yes, that's the only issue really,' said Craven sharply. 'Because of the takeover we have to make sure the figures are right. Keith thought they were.' He paused then turned back in his chair to face his desk. 'Sorry to be brief, but I've got a meeting at ten. All you need to know is in the file.' The conversation was over.

Mackay remained motionless, determined to have the last word after his abrupt dismissal. 'What's the address?' he said evenly.

'Sarah's got it,' came the irritated reply.

After a brief pause, Mackay left the room.

Mackay got the address from Sarah, Craven's secretary, and caught a cab to Connaught Lane, a narrow street off Buckingham Palace Road. He saw that Caspian House was a spacious, red-brick Victorian terraced house with a 1960s extension running southwards along the length of the street.

As Mackay got out of the cab, he saw that the police had cordoned off the far end of the street and that a large section of the multi-storey car park wall, where Mackay guessed Platt had met his end, was tented off. He signed in with the slovenly-looking security guard at the front desk and caught the lift to the third floor. There was no receptionist, so he went through the dark pine double doors opposite the lift.

The room he entered was the entire floor set out in open plan, most of the staff seated in one of two large rectangles. At the far end were three glass-partitioned rooms, the largest of which was clearly the boardroom. As he walked towards it, he was met with several inquisitive stares from bored staffers – a new face providing a welcome break from the tedium.

A middle-aged woman who sat outside the smaller office adjacent to the boardroom spoke to him as he approached the door.

'Are you from Blake and Lander?' she said gently.

Mackay half-smiled. 'Yes.'

She shook her head. 'Dreadful business, just dreadful.' She paused, then gestured to the boardroom. 'Keith used that room. His files are in the locked cupboard to the right of the flip chart.'

'Thanks. Where's the key?' asked Mackay politely.

'I don't know. I assume Keith must've taken it away with him on Friday night.' She paused. 'Do you want me to track down the master?'

'Thanks, just give me five minutes to look for it first. I'm Tom Mackay by the way.'

'June Paterson,' she replied, glancing at her monitor. 'Jonathan will be in shortly and it's possible the police might want a word with you.'

'OK,' said Mackay, making his way into the boardroom.

A quick check of the cupboard confirmed that it was locked and a cursory scan of the room didn't reveal the whereabouts of the key. He picked up the phone and called Erica, his departmental secretary.

'Erica Quirke,' she answered.

'Hi, it's me. Can you do us a quick favour?' There was an easy familiarity between them, which hadn't been spoilt by a drunken encounter one Friday night.

'Have you heard, Tom?'

'About Keith, you mean? Yeah, I'm out at his client now, there's police everywhere. Any sign of Sally yet?'

'She's in. No one knows what to say to her. Even the boss is lost for words.'

'Poor lass, it's all a bit unreal.' Mackay allowed a decent pause before changing subject. 'Can you find out who the junior was on this Caspian job and get them to call me out here?'

'Will do, Tom. Anything else?'

'No, that's it. Thanks. Bye, Erica.'

'Bye, Tom.'

Mackay thought about the distressed Sally Purcell. For sure she would be upset but Mackay had sensed that she and Platt had been drifting apart. How Platt had bedded her had been the shock of the year. She *was* the department looker with the body to match. Now she was alone and unattached. Mackay felt guilty and his mercenary thinking was interrupted by the phone.

It was Kyle Jones. If Mackay was the worst audit manager in the department, Kyle Jones was the worst junior. They were the two founder members of the department's awkward squad – shop stewards in all but name.

'What the hell do you want,' said Jones, in his usual respectful manner. 'You looking through my files to see if you can learn something about ticking and bashing?'

'It would help if I could get the pile of shite that you call audit work out of a locked cupboard. No wonder Platt threw himself under a car. I wouldn't fancy reviewing your files.'

'Oh that's nasty,' said Jones with a chuckle, 'and completely inappropriate humour. Have you no shame?' Jones paused. 'Try the hollow tube at the top of the flip chart. The black bung thing comes out on the right.' Mackay pulled the phone cable as far as it would go then reached over to the chart. There was no key, but the jarring had dislodged something metallic at the other end. He replaced the right-hand bung and popped out the left. The key fell into his hand.

'It's on the left-hand side, you twat,' said Mackay. 'Don't you Welshmen know your left from your right yet?'

'Not my fault dear old Keithy got himself confused.' Jones paused. 'And Tommy Boy?'

'What?' replied Mackay, dreading what was coming next.

'You can keep your filthy hands off the nubile Miss Purcell. What she needs now to cheer herself up is a taste of the Valleys.'

'Have you no shame...' began Mackay, but Jones had already hung up.

Mackay got the files out of the cupboard, opened the lead file, and began to read Jones's near illegible but artistic-looking scribble. As he worked his way through the balance sheet and profit-and-loss account schedules, he occasionally noticed Platt's neat handwriting giving further comments - why had the stationary expenses doubled, and why had the cleaning costs soared during the year?

Mackay yawned. Such was the riveting world of audit, he thought. Still, it warranted large fees, enabled him to pay his mortgage, and justified Craven's fifty-foot yacht.

Reading through the files, what really surprised Mackay was that Platt hadn't left a 'To Do List'. In all the years they had worked together, first when Platt had been Mackay's junior, then, following Platt's promotion, when they had been forced to share an office, he'd never known him not to leave a 'To Do List'. Indeed, it had been one of Mackay's pet hates.

Sometimes, on the rare occasions when Platt left the office before him, Mackay had sought out the 'To Do List' and added juvenile action points at the bottom, such as 'Lick Silas's arse,' or 'Shag Sally tonight'.

Had he been jealous of Platt? Perhaps, but Platt was dead. His life's 'To Do List' was irreversibly incomplete.

CHAPTER FIVE

Tuesday 22 April 1997

MAJOR OFFERS ALL STATE SCHOOLS FULL CONTROL
IRA BRINGS LONDON TO A STANDSTILL
RUTHLESS HODDLE DROPS JAMES

Despite privatisation, most of the rolling stock at King's Cross was still decked out in BR's old blue and yellow Intercity colours. Steadman's train, on the other hand, as befitted the new holder of the east coast franchise, had dark blue carriages with a thin red stripe running the length of the train through gold emblazoned GNER lettering.

A fresh coat of paint and a new brand - would that make a difference to Britain's railways? thought Steadman. He was hopeful that it would, though, for him, the awful almond-tasting coffee and forty-minute stop outside Stevenage wasn't a good start.

Despite the coffee, the hot carriage and last night's wine soon began to make him feel drowsy. When the middle-aged woman diagonally opposite him got off at Peterborough, he was able to stretch out fully and fall asleep.

He drifted in and out of sleep for the next three hours, vaguely conscious of the greater harshness in the accents of his fellow travellers and the greyness of the landscape. At Newcastle, his arrival in the north was confirmed when the train rattled slowly across a bridge over the Tyne.

Downriver, Steadman could see row upon row of red-brick terraced housing interspersed with crumbling factories, docks and warehouses. If Britain was booming, there was no sign of it here. The place had more in common with Brezhnev's USSR or Ceacescu's Bucharest than with Putney or Barnes. It was no doubt politically closer too, and, as in Eastern Europe, the voters had been powerless for years. Eighteen years in fact, but that would change next week.

Steadman wasn't looking forward to getting out of the train and nosing around. This was not his environment. He didn't feel comfortable and he doubted whether anyone was going to help him. This didn't feel like England to him.

Steadman had heard that one of the reasons why the Scots as a race were so cohesive was because a man from Dumfries could readily identify with a man from Inverness, despite living at the other end of the country. He doubted whether many folk on this train had much in common with him, never mind someone from Exeter. This felt like a foreign, hostile country.

About fifteen minutes north of Newcastle, the greys started to turn to greens and yellows, the urban hardness giving way to a softer rural landscape. As the train powered on, Steadman began to catch glimpses of the coast. He could see that the North Sea was bordered by very long stretches of golden sand, often curving round wide open bays, frequently ending with a rocky headland topped with a castle or ancient watch tower.

After a long right-hand bend, Steadman saw what he thought must be Alnmouth. In the distance he could see the town's red-brick houses, with their ochre pantile roofs, in elevated positions above a tiny golden estuary. Stunning, he thought, as the train gently braked and began to slow.

As Steadman was the only passenger to get off the train, the grey-whiskered station master, who had waved a green flag to dispatch the express on its way to Scotland, smiled at him warmly and said, 'Come far, sir?'

Steadman returned the smile. 'London.'

The station master nodded. 'Thought so. You look like you need a bit of a holiday.'

'Oh, I'll take it easy then,' said Steadman convivially. He paused. 'Any chance of getting a cab into town?'

'You'll have to call one from Alnwick so you're best off walking. It's only a mile. Go across the footbridge to the southbound platform and walk up the side of the hill from there. Make sure you stay in the Schooner Hotel. It does the best crab soup on the east coast.'

'OK, I will. Thanks.'

As Steadman crossed the footbridge, he observed that the Victorian station had a Railway Children feel to it, complete with hanging baskets filled with geraniums and lobelias, and freshly painted benches. He imagined the station master, brush in hand, sprucing up the benches every second Sunday in the month, while, in order to tend to the hanging baskets, his grey-haired wife undertook the more perilous stepladder work.

As he began to walk towards the town, Steadman was glad that the freshness of the sea air was partially offset by the weak April sun. After ten minutes of walking, the next headland past the town came into view, and he could see the ruins of a huge castle about a mile further on.

Steadman could see why the medieval builders had built it where they had. The castle was in a great defensive position, surrounded by sea on three sides. The narrow approach from the south was the only land link. He could see that the massive external walls of the main gatehouse were still largely intact, as were two towers to the north, but the rest of the walls had disappeared into the sea.

In a former life, the Schooner Hotel had been a coaching inn, and it was through the archway that coaches once rattled that Steadman made his way to reception. The room was empty, so he rang the brass bell and waited.

He glanced casually over the hotel's promotional literature, which lay strewn across the desk, noting numerous pictures of the castle he'd just seen. He saw that the fortification was called Dunstanburgh Castle, which had been built in the thirteenth century to keep out the Scots. Until then, it hadn't occurred to Steadman that where he stood was in the middle of Border country, where, only 400 years ago, there had been a real need for thick walls and iron gates.

Steadman rang the bell again. This time, the sound initiated a shuffling noise from the small room behind the desk.

'Can I help you?' said a female voice with a faint 'please piss off' tone. The voice intrigued him, and, when its owner appeared, he was not disappointed. She was in her late thirties, smallish, with a splash of long peroxide hair - the bleach was fading and failed to hide her roots. Her face was a bad Jerry Hall/Ulrika Jonsson mix, and, except for the blue T-shirt that she wore over her black skirt, she was quite definitely out of the Bet Lynch School of barmaids circa 1979. Indeed, she wore so much makeup that Steadman thought submersing her would lead to a small oil slick. He hoped she would be behind the bar that evening, sensing that she was single.

'Have you got a room for the night?' he asked politely.

'Only thirty,' she replied, without a flicker of a smile. 'Just the one night, is it?'

'Yeah. What's the rate?'

'Sixty quid. That includes breakfast.'

Her lack of warmth suggested that she was not the proprietor of the hotel but the hired help. The row upon row of keys lined up in a lockable cupboard behind the desk confirmed that the hotel was empty, but there was no reason why there'd been no attempt to sell him a room with a sea view, which he'd earlier noticed warranted a £75 tariff.

'Any chance of a sea view?'

'You having a romantic holiday on your own then?' she said with sarcastic humour.

'No, I'm working,' he replied nonchalantly. 'I'm a hot-shot journalist up from London investigating a national scoop.'

She eyed him more carefully, wondering whether he was serious, arrogant or both. 'Do you work for a tabloid then?'

He noted that the 'please piss off tone' had gone. 'Sort of.' He paused. 'You always lived in Alnmouth?'

'Born and bred. Not much happens round here that I don't hear of, I've worked in this bar far too long and there's not much village gossip that doesn't pass through it.' She half-smiled at him. 'Go on then. Ask me a question.'

'Well, it's a guy called Silas Craven I'm investigating. All I know is that he was married here about twenty years ago, to a woman called Penny Gray. Not much to go on.'

'Never heard of the bloke.' She hesitated. 'But the woman could be something to do with Gray Estates.' Warming to the subject, she added, 'there's a big house over by the castle called Branaff Hall, they used to have that but it's owned by the National Trust now. It might be worth you calling in there and getting hold of the guide, it's just opened for the season.'

'Thanks. That's very helpful.' He smiled at her and she smiled back, confirming a flicker of sexual attraction. 'You on all day?' he asked.

''Fraid so, front of house, the bar, the phone, what's it called, the latest buzz word they've got…multi-skilling.' She turned and reached for a key out of the lockable cupboard and handed it to Steadman. 'Through the door to the right and up the stairs to the second floor, room 207, breakfast's seven'til nine thirty and the bar serves meals 'til nine tonight, unless you want the restaurant that is.'

He was disappointed she hadn't offered to show him the room herself. 'No, the bar will be fine,' he said, picking up his suitcase. 'Thanks again.'

A National Trust leaflet that he nabbed on his way back through reception twenty minutes later revealed that Branaff Hall was at the north-westerly edge of the village, about half a mile from the Schooner. He set off at once and arrived just as the hall was opening.

He saw that the building was Jacobean and still had its original mullioned windows and arched porch, though the fortified square tower at its heart suggested that the present house was built on top of an earlier defensive structure. The visitor entrance was through the servants' quarters at the back of the hall. He bought a ticket and a guide and realised that, apart from a family of Dutch tourists, he had the house to himself. This enabled him to quiz the room stewards in a leisurely way about anything they might know about the Grays.

Steadman's £4 guide gave him a brief history of the Grays and described their history as an established Border Reiver family charged with maintaining law and order this side of the border prior to the Union of the Crowns. The family's fortunes ebbed and flowed with the fate of the Stuarts, but decline had become irreversible after the 1745 rebellion and a subsequent lengthy exile, which had seen the management of the estate neglected. On the present family there was little. The National Trust had taken over the house in the mid-seventies in lieu of death duties and there was no clue as to who the living Grays were or where they now lived.

Despairing that his visit had been a waste of time, Steadman walked towards the more-elderly-than-most female steward in the final room of the tour, the library. She was very old, in her late eighties or early nineties, and he saw that her movements were very slow and deliberate. She sat in the centre of the main library window and seemed to be both looking out to sea and reading her red leather book at the same time. She appeared not to notice Steadman's approach but a minute, feline-like adjustment of her head indicated that she was aware of his presence.

'Great view,' said Steadman with a smile. 'Do you really get paid to look out to sea all day? Don't fancy a job swap, do you?'

'Yes, I love sitting here,' she said weakly, half-turning towards him and looking him full in the face. 'The best views are first thing in the morning when the sun's behind the castle.'

Steadman was astonished by the intensity of her gaze and the sharpness of her green eyes. He felt as though she was assessing him from head to toe while she spoke, and he shifted his weight self-consciously from one leg to the other. 'This would have made a great family home in its day,' he said cautiously. 'The family were called the Grays, weren't they?'

'Yes,' she replied. 'They lived in this house for centuries, and before that in Dunstanburgh itself. They survived the Scots, Butcher Cumberland's Dragoons and even the Inland Revenue, all until about thirty years ago, when they died out after a serious of tragedies.' She paused. Steadman felt that she wanted to tell him more, and he was certainly keen to find out more about the series of tragedies.

'Oh, what were they?' he inquired innocently. 'The tragedies, I mean.'

She moved in her chair into what Steadman suspected was her storytelling position and closed her book. 'Well,' she said, looking at him intently again, ensuring that she had his full attention, 'Basil Gray died without issue in 1975 of a heart attack according to the doctors, but more like a broken heart in my view, considering what had gone on a few years earlier.' She hesitated and waited for him to ask what had gone on a few years earlier.

'What went on a few years earlier?' he dutifully asked.

'Well,' she said slowly, rolling the word around her lips, enjoying her control over his anticipation. 'Basil had two children, David and Penelope. Both died within two weeks of each other.' She paused, then stared at him intently so that her hidden meaning was clear. 'Both in tragic circumstances.' She hesitated again. He looked at her luminous green eyes, then she continued. 'Have you walked the cliff path by the side of the castle?'

'No,' he said.

'It's treacherous, very, very treacherous. In fact on a dark windy night when it's raining heavily and there's no moon, whole companies of Dragoons have been known to simply fall off it and go crashing down to their deaths on Greymare Rocks. That's what they say happened to Penelope Gray. Fell off the cliff to her death.'

Falling off cliffs and other such tragedies that cut life short were journalists' bread and butter. Steadman felt sure that the readers of the Borough Gazette would be interested. 'And the brother?' he asked. 'What happened to him?'

'Same thing,' replied the old woman, 'but on a tractor.'

'What?'

'If you walk along the path you'll see that the estate runs down to where the castle's moat was. There's a steep hill on the north side and a tractor with defective brakes is likely to go over the edge, which it did.' She paused. 'With David Gray on it.'

'Blimey,' said the journalist, 'my readers will be interested in this.' Steadman had decided to come clean and reveal the purpose of his visit to Branaff. The old woman had been keen to talk, and there was no reason to believe she wouldn't continue to do so.

'You writing a book about the Grays?' she said aggressively. Steadman instantly regretted his decision to be open. Some people simply didn't like talking to journalists.

'No,' he replied defensively. 'I'm a journalist investigating Penelope Gray's husband.'

The old woman threw herself out of the chair and at Steadman with such energy that he half-thought she might knock him over.

'Craven!' she said passionately.

At that moment, the family of Dutch tourists entered the room and she looked at them warily.

'Listen,' she said, grabbing his arm and drawing him in closer to her so that Steadman had to dip his head to hear. 'Let's not talk here. I'm out tonight, but come to Keeper's Cottage tomorrow morning at ten. It's the last house in the village just before the start of the castle path. I'll tell you what really happened to the Grays. I'm Anne Gill.'

Clearly exhausted by her exertions, she sank backwards and picked up her book, signalling that it was time for him to go.

'OK,' he said. 'I'm Nick Steadman. I'll see you tomorrow at ten.' They briefly looked at each other and he smiled at her. She acknowledged it and turned to the window.

Rather than head back to the Schooner straight away, Steadman decided to make the most of the fine weather and take the cliff path by the side of the castle. As he walked, he thought of Anne Gill and how excited she had become at the mention of Craven's name – the half-senile reaction of an old woman or something more?

He soon reached the castle and saw a large hazard sign in the National Trust's distinctive green lettering. The sign warned latter-day besiegers of the natural dangers of steep cliffs and slippery rocks, but didn't mention the man-made perils of barbed arrows and boiling oil that ancient besiegers had faced. Steadman's assumption that the warning only applied to elderly ramblers was quickly dispelled when the path suddenly narrowed to a few feet, squeezed between the wall and the cliff edge.

About fifty metres further on, at the point where cliff and wall became one, the path turned a sharp left into the fortress itself and continued through a series of deep internal trenches until it reached a natural well-like hole in the centre of the castle. Sea spray frothed and boiled up its sides and spurted out with a force worthy of an Eastern Bloc water cannon.

As he walked further north, Steadman was struck again by the stunning beauty of the coastline. In the far distance he could just make out a small island, which had at its centre a triangle-shaped rock with a castle on top.

'That's Holy Island,' said a gruff voice from behind him. 'That'll be where St Aidan first brought Christianity to these shores.' Steadman turned and looked at the speaker. The man had a blue peaked cap of the Uncle Albert style and a nautical look to him. He was in his late sixties or early seventies, trim looking but unshaven.

'Really?' said Steadman, with fake enthusiasm, the words 'I thought it was St Columba' dying on his lips. 'Where does the ferry go from? I quite fancy going across.'

'No ferry needed,' said the man. 'You can drive across the causeway from mid-morning 'til late afternoon at the moment. I'd check the exact times with the tourist office though if I were you.' The man continued to mouth something at Steadman but a huge column of water firing up through the block-hole separated sound from words, so Steadman smiled at the man, nodded his head and turned back towards Alnmouth.

Steadman returned to the Schooner and rang the bell. There was the expected delay and the standard 'Can I help you?' in the same 'please piss off' tone he'd heard earlier. Moments later, the receptionist appeared from the small ante-room. She smiled at him in a personal rather than commercial way.

He returned her smile. 'Sorry to bother you again. Any chance I could borrow your phone book?'

She turned to the table behind her, giving Steadman a brief opportunity to study her figure. Where his girlfriend Shannon was thin and slight, she was fleshy and ample - in reasonable shape, yes, but no one would describe her as lean. Steadman found himself irresistibly drawn to her. She sensed this when she spun back to the desk and caught him gawping at her.

A look of amusement crossed her face. 'Here,' she said, handing him the book.

He reached out for it, suddenly terrified that he might touch her hand. 'Thanks,' he mumbled, surprised at his lack of confidence.

'Just pop it back on the desk when you've finished with it.' She smiled at him again and he smiled back at her like an awkward adolescent.

'Is it possible to get a drink round here?' shouted a voice from the bar.

She left and Steadman began to leaf through the pages. There was only one Craven in the book, M. Craven, listed at the Dower House, Berwick Street. He had noticed Berwick Street on his way to Branaff Hall earlier in the day, so, after returning the book to reception, he set off.

The Dower House was a regency building, chunky looking, with large square windows and the distinctive Northumberland arch that Steadman had seen on several houses in the town. He knocked at the door, which opened slowly to reveal a small, grey, sprightly-looking woman.

'Yes?' she said.

'Mrs Craven?' he asked softly.

'Yes,' she repeated, with a trace of apprehension.

'My name's Nick Steadman. I'm a journalist from a paper in London covering the election in Wandsworth, where your son's standing.'

'Yes,' she said for a third time, with a relieved look. 'How can I help you?'

'Well, I'm just researching a bit on all the candidates, their backgrounds, where they come from, that sort of thing. It's important that our readers get to feel that they know the candidates well. After all, it's their votes that will count on Thursday.'

She hesitated, clearly torn between her maternal desire to talk about her son and her intuitive wariness of journalists. 'I'd...' she paused, still internally debating, then she continued firmly, her mind made up. 'I'd better check with Silas first if you don't mind. Please come in while I call him. Which paper did you say you were from?'

'The Borough Gazette. By all means call him, Mrs Craven.'

Steadman was ushered into a pale green drawing room where he sat down and waited. He heard Mrs Craven speaking to someone on the phone. He suspected that he would soon be leaving. He doubted that Craven would consent to his interviewing his mother. Indeed, it was likely that Craven would react badly when he discovered there was a journalist sniffing around his hometown.

Steadman looked around the room and saw several pictures of Craven. Craven as a baby, Craven in school uniform, a youthful-looking Craven with a young woman, both dressed in the full 'Shooting Life' uniform, and, finally, Craven as Steadman had seen him a few days ago, only this time in his Sloane Square gear, this time with a more sophisticated-looking woman on his arm.

Steadman hadn't heard Mrs Craven come back into the room, so he was startled when she spoke to him from behind. 'I can't get hold of him,' she said. 'His secretary thinks he's somewhere in Fulham.' She walked to the fireplace and sat down in the comfortable-looking armchair opposite him. 'What would you like to know?'

Steadman was relieved. 'Well, just a bit about his early life in Alnmouth, his career, family life, a pen portrait really. Talking me through those photos might be a good start.'

'OK,' she said, with no sign of her earlier reservations. 'Let me put the kettle on and I'll tell you all about them.'

Steadman sat through half an hour of a detailed and dull account of Craven's childhood. As an only child, his mother had been devoted to him, especially after Craven's father had been killed in a mining accident in nearby Ashington Colliery. Steadman was surprised to discover that Craven's father had been a miner, though Mrs Craven was keen to stress on several occasions that, although he'd started out as a miner, he'd soon been promoted to foreman.

She had tried to be a loving mother, but bringing up a child on a paltry widow's pension had been tough, and it was not until she'd secured a position as housekeeper at Branaff Hall that things had got better. The squire, Basil Gray, immediately took to Silas, developing him over the years and getting him his accountancy articles at a local firm. Once Silas had qualified, Gray then used his connections to smooth his entry into the City.

The road from working-class mining family in Ashington to the Tory Party candidate for Barnes and West Putney was a long and unusual one, thought Steadman, and the irony that Mrs Craven now lived in the estate's Dower House, while the hoi polloi roamed freely over the hall itself, was not lost on him.

'Who's that?' said Steadman, pointing at the 'Shooting Life' picture of Steadman and the young woman.

'Penny Gray,' she said with a sigh, 'Silas's first wife and Basil's daughter. She fell on the cliff path, a terrible accident.' She paused. 'They were so well suited.'

A touch of the Wuthering Heights about this tale, thought Steadman. 'Tragic,' he said, as empathetically as he could.

It was clear Mrs Craven had exhausted her usefulness and he was keen to further investigate Penny Grays's accident, so, after a few minutes of small talk, he made his excuses and left.

He called in at the library then returned to his room at the Schooner, disappointed to find the reception empty as he passed through. He had a bath and went down to the bar for supper. The bar would have been described as a nautically themed pub in London, with the seafaring kit hanging from its walls made in an industrial estate in Slough (circa 1995), except that, because the Schooner had served mariners from Alnmouth's small port for centuries, the pictures of sailing ships, browning pennants, old fraying ropes and rusted anchors were genuine.

Steadman ordered his food and settled into a severe-looking wooden booth by the fire. He flicked through the back issues of the Northumberland Journal that he'd photocopied in the library. After about ten minutes, he found what he was looking for.

7 May 1969
Northumberland Journal

LOCAL LANDOWNER'S DAUGHTER KILLED IN CLIFF FACE ACCIDENT

Penny Craven, daughter of Basil Gray of Branaff Hall, was killed on Saturday while walking the coastal path near Dunstanburgh Castle. It is believed Mrs Craven lost her footing in the dark and fell off the cliff while walking her dog.

Nothing new there, thought Steadman, as he eyed up the incoming tray the barman was carrying. He was hungry, so the crab soup and lasagne were going to taste good, and the beer was going to be thirst quenching.

It was still early and the bar was empty when the shift changed. Steadman was pleased when the barman was relieved by the blonde receptionist, and he was delighted when she smiled at him when she picked his tray.

He gulped down the remainder of his pint and was halfway out of his seat and heading for the bar stool nearest to the pumps, ready to try his hand, when the blue peaked cap man of the Uncle Albert style, whom he'd briefly met at the castle, edged in beside him.

'You don't mind if I join you?' he said, almost to himself. 'Enjoy your walk then?' The second question, unlike the first, invited some sort of response from Steadman, so he nodded.

There was a lengthy pause as both men looked at Steadman's empty pint glass. Steadman gave in first. 'Can I get you a drink?' he said.

'Well, only if you're having one anyway,' came the eager reply. 'I'll have a pint of Federation.'

Steadman went to the bar to get the drinks. 'Two pints of that please,' he said to the receptionist, pointing to the Federation pump, 'and one for yourself.'

'That's very kind,' she purred, beginning to pour the pints. 'I see Old Joe's latched on to you. Don't worry, he's harmless enough. Must say it's quite unusual for him to pick on a stranger like that though.'

'I met him up at the castle. He told me a bit about Holy Island.'

'That explains it, that's just his taster. You'll get the full history now.' She finished pouring the pints and then handed him the frothy glasses.

'Thanks,' he said, looking her directly in the eye. 'I didn't catch your name earlier.'

'Judith,' she said, holding his stare.

He glanced away. 'Thanks, Judith.'

Steadman returned to the booth and put Old Joe's pint in front of him.

'Your good health,' the old man said warmly, 'and mine' – the thought no doubt triggered by their difference in age. The old man looked at the bar, then spoke softly in a conspiratorial tone. 'She's single, our Judith, you know.'

'Really?' replied Steadman, in the most disinterested tone he could manage.

'Never been married,' said the self-appointed old matchmaker, who was encouraged by Steadman's neutral response. 'That's not to say she hasn't had her admirers though.' Steadman looked at him more closely to gauge his meaning and noticed the Sid James twinkle in his eye. 'Quite a few fellas she's been…er...involved with, all of 'em bad sorts. Time for her to settle down now, I say.'

'I'll bear that in mind,' said Steadman. He paused, then changed the subject. 'You lived in Alnmouth long?'

'All my life,' said Joe, effortlessly switching from local matchmaker to village sage.

Steadman detected the change. Here was an opportunity to get the old man's slant on the demise of the Grays. 'I was at the hall today,' he began cautiously. 'Much as I admire the work of the Trust, I always think it's a shame to see these old houses turned from homes into museums. Pretty tragic end to the family that lived there I was hearing.'

Joe's eyes lit up and he glanced quickly from side to side in much the same way as Rene would have done, had the Schooner been instantly transported back in time to Vichy France. Steadman heard the bar door open behind him and he turned to look, half-expecting Herr Flick to walk through it, but instead it was the Dutch tourists he'd seen at the hall earlier in the day.

'No tragedy about it,' said the old man, drawing closer to Steadman. 'A family curse, started in the seventeenth century by Edmund Gray, warden of the English East March.'

'Warden of the English East March?' repeated Steadman. 'What's that?'

'Well,' said Joe, relishing the question, 'before the Union of the Crowns in 1603 the area round here was Border country, a long way from London and the authority of the English queen, and a long way from Edinburgh and the Scottish king. A lot of thieving went on at full moon, especially of cattle. This was known as "Riding" or "Reiving". The closer to the border you were the more lawless and barbaric it got.'

Joe paused for breath, then continued. 'Folk belonged to a family or clan and they stuck together, aiding fellow clan members if they got into trouble. Ancient blood feuds were common. In order to keep some sort of law and order, both monarchs appointed three wardens and the border territory was divided into the East, Middle and West Marches. Of course, offences committed in their own marches could be dealt with by their own courts but wardens on both sides of the border couldn't deal with criminals from the opposite march, who often stole cattle then fled to the other side of the border.'

Joe took a sip of his pint, then continued, 'To deal with the problem, wardens agreed to meet their opposite wardens on "days of truce", where those attending had safe conduct from sunrise to sunset in the appointed town. Having given assurances to each other about the truce, they would then form a jury of six Scottish gentlemen appointed by the Scottish warden and six English gentlemen appointed by the English warden. This jury tried the Reivers. The "days of truce" became a sort of bank holiday fair, where hawkers and tinkers would set up their stalls and all would have a gay time, except of course the convicted Reivers, who were hanged.'

'What's all this got to do with the Grays?' asked Steadman.

'Well, the problem with the system was that the March Lords were often drawn from the border families, so impartiality and the objective dispensing of justice could prove difficult. The wardens were the biggest crooks of all. Their office was seen as a way of enriching themselves and their families, a gift for services rendered to the queen, which in the case of the Grays was unusual, because they were Catholics. For a long time the patronage of the queen ensured their protection from their ancient blood enemies, the Taits, and in particular Willie Tait, warden of the Scottish East March.'

Old Joe finished his pint and Steadman was sent to the bar for refills. He saw that it was dark outside now and that the bar was full, the patrons drawn to the blazing log fire, which threw its light out onto the road in sharp red and orange tongues. He was eager to hear the next instalment of Joe's story, so he smiled at rather than spoke to Judith as she pulled the next round. He returned to the booth. 'We'd got as far as the Taits,' he said.

Joe grabbed the pint as if playing Hungry Hippos and took a long draught as if he'd been a month in a desert. 'Well, it was late March 1603 when the "day of truce" was called and it was agreed that it would be held in the small market town of Calder. Now, Edmund Gray was determined to get even with Willie Tait, seeing as he'd hanged one of his own cousins as a Reiver the year before, and it was fortunate for Gray that, as he journeyed to Calder, he met Sir Robert Carey, who was on his way to Edinburgh to fetch King James down to London as Queen Elizabeth's successor. Fearing an end to the system and his own position, Edmund decided to act. The next day, Willie Tait and his retainers arrived in Calder assuming they'd be guaranteed safe passage, but, unaware of the queen's death, they were all taken by surprise and hanged on trumped up charges of treason.'

'But weren't the Grays punished by King James?' said Steadman.

Joe half-laughed. 'No, the king was unsure of his own position at the beginning of his reign, and by the time he'd established himself he'd become so anglicised that he'd forgotten all about his Scottish nobles. He never returned to Scotland once during his reign you know. But as Willie Tait stood there on the gallows waiting for the drop, he looked at Edmund Gray and cursed him and his family."The Grays shall never grow grey," he shouted at the crowd. And that's how it's been – no male members of the family have ever reached fifty. Cursed they've been from that day to this, and now they're all gone. Basil Gray was the last – died of a broken heart about twenty years ago after his son and daughter died on Greymare Rocks, just below where I met you today. Tragedy some say, cursed I say.'

Steadman nodded. The yarn was over. They continued to talk about Alnmouth life in general and how it compared to London living, about Joe's time on the boats and about journalism.

It became clear that there was nothing new on Craven and Steadman noticed that it was an hour before closing time. He saw that the stool he'd set off for earlier was still free, so a late sortie to the bar was still an option. With Joe's blessing, he moved to the bar and sat himself down on the stool. His intent was clear, and Judith read the signals. As none of the customers were close to ordering a drink, she picked up the large gin and tonic she'd hidden behind the till, came round to the customers' side of the bar and sat down beside him.

'You come here often?' he said humorously, with a Roger Moore raised eyebrow and a silly smile. She laughed, and, when the bar had emptied, they were still talking.

CHAPTER SIX

Wednesday 23 April 1997

MAJOR INSISTS TORIES CAN STILL WIN
POLL SHOWS LABOUR FIFTEEN POINTS CLEAR
HESELTINE CALLS POLLSTERS CLOWNS

Mackay had a phone next to his bed. If it hadn't been by his bed when it rang at 7.30 that morning, it would have gone unanswered. The voice on the other end of the line was clearly a native English speaker but the accent was strange, and Mackay was unable to place it.

'Thomas Mackay?' said the voice in an officious tone.

'Yes,' he replied apprehensively.

'Thomas Mackay of 17D Garlieston Street, Putney, London?'

'Yes, can I help you?' said Mackay quickly, in a way that suggested he was beginning to wonder whether the caller was some sort of foreign law enforcement officer – Interpol perhaps.

The caller continued in the same flat tone. 'Mr Mackay, my name is John Benady. I'm a partner in the firm of Likudi, Benady, Gomez and Scott solicitors, here in Gibraltar. I do apologise for calling at such an early hour. However, I wanted to try and catch you before you went to work as I don't have your work number.'

Mackay was intrigued. What did this lawyer want with him? He'd never been to Gibraltar before. 'How can I help you?' he repeated.

'Mr Mackay, I'm afraid I've some very bad news. Your uncle, Joe Sharp, sadly passed away yesterday.' Benady paused to let the news sink in and then waited for a sign of surprise, shock or early grief. As there was only silence, he continued with the same measured calmness in his voice. 'The reason for my call, Mr Mackay, is that your uncle's will, which I have here in front of me, appoints you and I as joint executors of his estate.'

'Where and what did he die of?' asked Mackay.

'A heart attack at his villa in Jimenez,' replied Benady. 'By the time the ambulance arrived, I gather that he'd already been dead for some time. It's unlikely that he suffered.'

Mackay imagined his uncle, clothed in his white Miami Vice-style jacket, lying dead by the pool in his spacious villa. 'That's the best we could hope for.' Mackay had been fond of his uncle, but he hadn't spoken to him for years. That his heart had failed after years of hard living was no surprise. 'What do we do now?'

'Well, the first thing is to get probate, then we can access his funds and begin discharging his liabilities. It's likely that getting to that stage will take a month or two. After that we can start distributing the estate to his beneficiaries.'

'Am I a beneficiary?' asked Mackay, a little too hurriedly.

'Yes, you, your sister and your other cousins get equal shares,' replied the solicitor.

'And the size of the estate?'

Benady hesitated. 'Difficult to put a precise figure on it. There's the villa in Jimenez, some property in the UK, shares and quite a lot of cash. Fortunately it was our firm that helped your uncle a few years ago when he ran into difficulty with the Inland Revenue.'

'More than a million then?' pressed Mackay.

'Forgive me, but it's not easy to be certain,' squirmed the lawyer. 'Property values, the shifting equity markets...'

Mackay interrupted and did his best to sound authoritative. 'Go on, what's your best guess?'

'I think a million pounds is as good an estimate as any at this stage,' replied the solicitor evenly. He paused, giving Mackay time to mix the genealogy with the arithmetic. 'The thing is, Mr Mackay, I really need your signature on a number of documents to get things moving as quickly as possible, plus it would be useful to have a thorough discussion with you about strategy in terms of asset disposals. Your uncle had a couple of investments, for example, which, even at this early stage, I would strongly recommend remain…' He hesitated, then continued in a soft conspiratorial tone, 'shall we say…offshore.'

There was a further pause as both men took stock of the conversation, Benady wondering whether he'd gone too far, and Mackay wondering whether 'offshore' might present opportunities for him that would be denied to his cousins.

It was Benady who spoke first. 'If you could spare the time, Mr Mackay, it might be worth you coming out to Gibraltar. It'll probably be more efficient spending half a day in the office here and signing all the documents at one sitting, rather than me sending over reams of documents in dribs and drabs and you sending them back. What do you think?'

Mackay knew that Ryanair and Easyjet were expanding rapidly but was pretty sure that the Gibraltar route still remained the preserve of British Airways. As a rule, unless the client was paying, lowly audit managers never paid for BA flights out of their own pockets, so the thought of paying his own way to get to Benady's office did not appeal.

Correctly sensing that Mackay's hesitation signalled reluctance, Benady continued, 'of course, your expenses would be met from the estate. Shall I see if I can book you into the Rock Hotel? It's starting to get busy at this time of year but I know the manager very well. In fact, why don't I see you in the office here first thing on Monday morning? You and your wife could fly out on Friday and make a weekend of it?'

Of course, there really was no comparison between the prospect of sunning himself in warm Mediterranean climes and another weekend spent trailing hopelessly around the Cresswell Estate, being berated by the likes of Headbutt and hounded by Butch, so Mackay readily consented and agreed to meet Benady at 9am on Monday morning at Linewall Road, Gibraltar.

As it wasn't yet eight, Mackay was tempted to have another twenty minutes in bed but then he remembered he was a professional and got up. He was in Victoria and at his desk within the hour, strangely motivated, though this energy soon began to leak away after an hour spent with the audit files.

The absence of Platt's 'To Do List' continued to irritate him, not only because it was unusual, but also because it meant he had to do a full re-review of the files himself, rather than just look at the outstanding bits that Platt had left.

The morning passed quickly and, after a liquidish lunch in the Duke of Connaught, Mackay decided to review the income file. After an hour, he saw some notes in pencil that Platt had made in the margins of one of the schedules. The writing had been rubbed out, but Mackay could still make out the words, 'Insurance rebate £7m,' which his predecessor had also underlined. This was odd because there was no 'Insurance rebate' caption shown in any of the lead or supporting schedules, nor could Mackay find any trace of it in any of the account balances that the computer had spewed out.

What sort of insurance did Caspian have? There was the usual buildings insurance, and employees' and directors' liability insurance, but these amounts were small and wouldn't have been material enough to warrant further investigation by Platt. Mackay decided to ask the MD what this rebate was at the first opportunity.

That opportunity came mid-afternoon, when Jonathan Bridger called him into his office. 'Please, come in Tom.'

Bridger used the open palm of his hand to invite Mackay to take the seat opposite his desk and sat down himself. He smiled at Mackay warmly and the auditor looked at his client more closely. He was in his fifties yet he still had a full head of tawny brown hair, which he combed to the side of his head with a touch of Brylcreem. Bridger was well over 6 ft, probably nearer 6 ft 3, and in good shape with just a hint of a banker's paunch. His face was hard lined, almost geometric. His plain dark blue suit was Jermyn Street, as was his plain pink shirt, but his blue tie had a small motif or shield in the centre of it, which Mackay took to represent membership of some exclusive Edinburgh Club - maybe the New Club.

'How's the audit going?' asked Bridger.

Mackay was surprised at the lack of opening pleasantries. 'Very well thanks, most of the work's been done already. Keith did a good job.'

'Yes, I thought he would. Struck me as a very thorough guy. A terrible shame.'

'Yes,' replied Mackay, 'it was.'

There was a long embarrassed silence.

Bridger spoke first. 'Is everyone being as helpful as they can? Just let me know if there's anything I can do.'

Mackay, like most of his profession, didn't like coming across awkward audit issues. His usual solution was to book himself on next year's audit as soon as possible, then leave the problem alone, hoping it would disappear by the time he revisited the books twelve months later.

Why then did he ask the following question? 'Well, Jonathan, there is one thing that's troubling me.'

'Oh, what's that?' replied the banker, sitting slightly back in his chair and clasping his hands together.

'Keith left notes indicating that Caspian was due a large insurance rebate of some kind. Do you know anything about it?'

Bridger's expression was blank. 'No, I don't,' he said. 'Have you tried Colin? He might know something about it.' Colin Brown was Caspian's financial controller.

'Yes, I'll ask him.'

The auditor and client looked at each other carefully. Mackay felt uncomfortable. Bridger's reply had been a bit too prepared and measured. Surely a more natural reaction would have been one of concern, or at least of further inquiry. On the other hand, perhaps he was being paranoid, and Brown did have an explanation for the rebate.

'If there's anything else you need, don't hesitate to ask,' said Bridger, with a salesman's smile.

Mackay got up to leave and headed for the door. After a couple of steps, he half-turned to face Bridger who'd been watching his exit.

'Oh, just in case you're wondering where I am on Monday, I'm having the day off.'

'Going somewhere nice for the weekend?' asked the banker.

'Gibraltar, to sort out my uncle's estate. He died yesterday.'

'I'm sorry to hear that.' Bridger left a decent pause. 'Were you close?'

'Not really. I haven't seen as much of him since he moved out to Spain. He was great fun when I was a kid though.'

'Well I know it's not a good time but try and make the most of The Rock – it's the best place the bank ever sent me, and the views from the summit on a fine day are the best in Europe.'

'OK, I will.' He looked at Bridger, who was staring blankly at him, still in the midst of nostalgia about his youth, and, for some reason, Mackay felt sorry for him.

Mackay returned to the boardroom and hurriedly packed up. Uniquely for him, and in accordance with standard audit practice, he locked the files away properly and took the key with him. It was late in the afternoon but, instead of calling it a day, he decided to return to the office. He picked up an early edition of the Standard and caught the next eastbound District Line train.

As the tube idled outside St James's Park, he glanced casually at the first few pages. The latest polls made grim reading. This election is a joke, thought Mackay. His absence from the Cresswell Estate frontline this weekend was going to make bugger all difference – Major was already yesterday's prime minister.

As the tube left St James's Park, Mackay was surprised that no one came to claim the suitcase resting on the other side of the partition from him. He looked round the carriage. Seated facing him was an Indian woman dressed from head to foot in black, and, to his right, were three shabbily dressed businessmen, all in creased grey suits. A middle-aged woman with badly dyed auburn hair in a bright green coat stood on his side of the carriage at the next door.

Mackay's decision to reclassify the suitcase from attended to unattended was driven by the fact that if it went off he would have the blast all to himself. Was he being paranoid? The suitcase did bother him. It had nearly toppled over after the last bend and any further lurches to the left might prove fatal.

He looked again around the carriage but none of his fellow travellers had any interest in the suitcase. In fact, the only response he got was a hostile glare from the Indian woman, who thought he was ogling her. He looked more closely at her, and noted that she did have an attractive Bollywood-type aura.

The carriage lurched to the left and the suitcase tipped thirty to forty degrees off its base then settled back against the partition. Mackay could feel his heart beating quickly and a cold sweat developing along his spine – there was nothing for it but to act.

'Is this anyone's suitcase?' he said, addressing the carriage in his best Scotland Yard voice. There was the usual, 'God I hope you're not speaking to me,' pause, which Londoners adopted when anyone spoke on public transport, but the implication of Mackay's question provoked a reaction from the three businessmen, who began to eye the suitcase nervously.

One of them shifted his gaze to Mackay and said, 'nothing to do with us mate.'

'It's mine,' came a welcome Antipodean cry from the door. It was the middle-aged woman with badly dyed auburn hair in the bright green coat, who walked along the aisle and casually took possession of the suitcase.

She smiled at Mackay as the train pulled into Westminster, picked up the suitcase and proceeded to get off. Having disembarked, she turned to Mackay and said with a cheeky look on her face, 'I'm off to blow up Parliament.'

'Make sure you get all of them,' he replied with a strained smile. The door closed and the tube set off towards Embankment.

Mackay got to the office without further incident and was glad to discover that he'd the room to himself, Tony King being out at a client. The insurance rebate still bothered him. If it was a rebate, then there had to have been previous payments and these must have been recorded.

He rang up the post room and commissioned a priority recall of the previous years' audit files. As the archived files were held offsite, he was told it would take an hour to get them, so he decided to use the time constructively in the Bell Inn on Fleet Street.

He put on his jacket and was about to leave when Sally Purcell stepped into his office.

'You OK?' he said, as sympathetically as he could manage.

'Fine, Tom,' she said quickly, sounding irritated. She saw he had his jacket on. 'You off somewhere?'

'I'm going down to the Bell for an hour or so.' He paused and smiled at her. 'Fancy a drink?'

She looked relieved. 'Only if it's a double. Come on.'

They found a secluded table in the bay of the pub's frosted glass window. Mackay ordered a double gin and tonic and a pint of London Pride.

'You're doing Keith's audit,' she said, as a neutral opener.

'Yes, not much to do on it. You know what he was like, pretty thorough.'

'Yes,' she replied.

Would she burst into tears at the mention of Platt's name? He doubted it. Mackay had been close to her a few years ago and they'd kissed once at an office party. There had been sexual chemistry there then but it had gone no further. They had remained kindred spirits though and shared a common bond of cynicism. Mackay had always been disappointed that their relationship had developed in a platonic way – he could not understand what she had seen in Platt.

'Listen, Tom, I'm glad I caught you in the office. I needed someone who understands me to talk to. My relationship with Keith was on its last legs and I'm sick of being the recipient of so much unwarranted sympathy. I was bored of him and I was going to dump him last Friday. There, I've said it.' She finished her drink in a single gulp and got up from the table. 'My round then.' She paused and looked at him. 'Same again?'

He was caught off balance by her unexpected revelation but he managed to splutter out. 'No, I'll try a Spitfire this time.' She turned and headed for the bar.

He took a large swig out of his glass while he waited for her return. He looked at her as she stood at the bar. She was petite, curvaceous and very attractive. Her hair was discreetly highlighted and loosely bobbed almost in a boyish way. Her mouth was irresistible, and her large blue eyes simply drew Mackay in. The way she spoke, her soft American drawl, he found intoxicating.

She returned with the drinks, and he put the empty glasses on the next table. They continued to talk and drink. They gossiped about people in the department, about the election and Mackay's escapades on the Cresswell Estate, at which she laughed, about his unsuccessful pursuit of Annabel, and about his worry about Craven's predatory behaviour towards her.

'Craven's an oily one,' said Sally, 'he was leching after me at a Christmas party a couple of years ago. I can see why some women go for him though.'

'Why's that, Sal?'

She thought for a moment, then continued. 'He kind of envelops you with quality, quality clothes, smells, gifts, cars. He makes you feel you'd be safe with him and well looked after. He gives you all the things you always wanted from your father, plus, he has the maturity a girl wants from a partner. He looks good and I bet he'd make a great lover.'

'Sounds like you've thought of him before in this light, Sal,' said Mackay teasingly. 'You sure nothing came of that Christmas party?'

She grinned. 'What, and then I fled into the arms of reliable, dull, old Keith when it all ended in tears?'

'Yeah, something like that.'

Her remark was light-hearted but Mackay couldn't help wondering whether there might be some truth in it. True or not, he didn't really care, just as long as she next fled into the arms of unreliable, stimulating, old Mackay.

'Listen, I know you won't believe this,' he said, 'but I've got to get back to the office. I've recalled some files from archives I fancy having a quick flick through before I head off.'

She was surprised. 'Most unlike you Tom,' she said. 'What's so important?'

'Oh nothing much, just a loose end from Keith's audit.'

'Well, why don't we have another drink, then I'll come up with you and we can go through them together.'

'Great,' he replied, startled by her offer of help, 'but why the sudden desire to join the evening audit shift?'

She got up and headed towards the bar. 'Don't worry,' she said, with her back to him, 'you'll be paying for dinner.'

He quickly finished his pint. Where the hell was this evening leading to?

Until their liability is limited by the seven-year period set by the Companies Act, all audit firms keep files covering their previous audits. Those files evidenced Blake and Lander's most important product, audit opinions. In theory, the files were all that stood between angry creditors and the partners' homes in Surrey if things ever went wrong. Things never did go wrong though, and, if they did, firms always settled rather than go to court, thereby avoiding any dangerous precedents that could be referred to later.

As Blake and Lander had won the Caspian audit in 1991, upwards of thirty files were stored in the four large boxes now sitting on Mackay's desk.

'What are we looking for, Tom?' asked Sally.

Mackay told her about Platt's notes indicating a £7 million insurance rebate of which there was now no trace. He also voiced his concerns about the absence of Platt's 'To Do List'.

'I'm sure there's a reasonable explanation for it, Sal. We'll no doubt find the answer in these boxes.' He paused. 'That's odd.'

'What is it, Tom?'

'Look, someone's had these boxes out recently.'

Underneath the gold 'B&L' emblazoned on each box was a red grid, which the archivists used to track where each box had been. In the 'out' column on all four boxes was the date 15 April 1997. In the 'In' column was the date 22 April 1997.

'Unusual that Keith took out all the old audit files,' continued Mackay. 'He must have been looking for this insurance thing as well.'

Mackay took out his keys and began cutting through the brown tape sealing each box. He suddenly stopped again. 'That's even more puzzling, Sal.'

She looked up from a box she was grappling with herself. 'What is, Tom?'

He glanced from one box to the next. 'These boxes were sent back to the archives a week after they were got out, on 22 April – yesterday.'

She was intrigued. 'What of it?'

'Question is who sent them back, Sal? Keith had been dead for five days.'

'I suppose he could have emailed instructions to Erica or one of the other girls,' she said unconvincingly.

He nodded. 'It's possible, I'll check tomorrow.' Of course, it was possible, but it wasn't likely. No one was that anal, not even Platt. Mackay began to feel uncomfortable about Caspian. Was there something sinister going on?

'Nothing in this box either,' said Sally an hour later. 'They're mostly balance sheet files.'

Mackay had also looked through his boxes without success. 1995, 1994, 1993: each file looked remarkably similar to the previous year. 'If the dates weren't different, Sal, you'd think some of these sheets were photocopies of earlier years.'

She laughed and said, 'why did the auditor cross the road?'

'Because she did it last year,' he replied with a smile. 'Thought you yanks didn't have a sense of humour?'

'You call audit jokes humorous?

'OK, point taken.'

Mackay turned back to the files in front of him. Every year, profits were ten per cent up on the year before, and every year there was a corresponding year end adjustment in the company's provisions, just to make sure that profit growth was nice and smooth.

Mackay smiled to himself as he flicked through the 1994 file. He saw that Caspian had had a bumper year and recorded profit before provisions of £14.4 million, a twenty per cent jump on the 1993 figure. The same year, a £1.2 million provision for redundancies had been booked, so the final profit figure submitted to Group had shown only a ten per cent increase year on year.

He picked up the 1995 file again, a poorer year, and saw that the profit before provisions had dropped to £12.5 million, but this had been OK because Jonathan Bridger had obviously felt that redundancies were not necessary after all, so the £1.2 million provision made the previous year, along with a further £1 million from some specific provisions, had been released to profit, meaning that the final figures released to Group showed a ten per cent increase in profits year on year.

'Sal, I bet Bridger's bonus is contingent on Caspian hitting ten per cent a year profit growth. Some of these provisions are a joke.'

'You seen who the partner's been since '91?' she replied.

'What, Craven?' he asked rhetorically. 'On the same job for six years. You're kidding? You really can't beat a bit of auditor independence,' he said sarcastically.

A few minutes later, Mackay began flicking through the 1991 file. He saw that in the general correspondence section, there was a letter from the Avon and General Insurance Company, which read as follows:

Avon and General Insurance
23-27 Bernard Street
Bristol
BS8 6NE
Tel. 0117 909 6000
Fax. 0117 909 6001

Jonathan Bridger
Managing Director
Caspian Credit Limited
No. 2 Connaught Lane
Victoria
London
SW1 7RQ

June 17, 1991

Dear Jonathan,

Master Credit Insurance - Policy No. CF/89/762
Further to our telephone conversation yesterday, I confirm that due to the low number of claims submitted under the terms of this policy, no further premiums are due.

Yours sincerely,

Angus Cook
Senior Underwriter

Mackay turned to the payments section of the file but discovered that the schedule dealing with insurance costs was missing.

'Look at this, Sal,' he said excitedly. 'Could be what we're looking for.' He showed her the letter and the missing costs page then continued, 'funny how there's no mention of Avon and General in any of the other files we've been through. Almost as if someone's been through them.'

'You see conspiracies everywhere,' she said flatly. 'I'm sure there's a perfectly sensible explanation.'

'Sal, I asked Bridger directly about this and he denied any knowledge of it.'

'Could be any number of reasons,' she said firmly, clearly determined to deflate his excitement. 'Let's call it a day and grab something to eat. I'm off to powder my nose and pack up my desk and I want you ready to go in ten minutes.' She lightly touched his arm and moved towards him just enough to enter his personal space.

'OK,' he said sheepishly.

Suggestion, request, instruction, command or decree - it made no difference if the words came from Sally Purcell's lips. There was an expectation that men would obey her and wish to please her - Mackay was no different.

She left the room and he hurried to the other side of his desk and picked up the phone. The number he called for Avon and General Insurance had changed, but, with the help of the operator, he got the new phone and fax numbers and was able to confirm that the company was still at the same address as it had been six years ago. Then he sat down at his desk and typed the following letter:

Blake and Lander
Sir Thomas More Square
Temple
London
EC6 7EB

Tel. 0171 552 8909
Fax. 0171 552 8910

Contact Tom Mackay
23 April 1997

Avon and General Insurance
23-27 Bernard Street
Bristol
BS8 6NE

Dear Sirs,

Caspian Credit Limited
Master Credit Insurance - Policy No. CF/89/762

As part of our audit procedures and in accordance with the instructions of our mutual client, Caspian Credit Limited, we would be grateful if you would fax to us at the earliest possible convenience copies of all the correspondence between yourselves and our mutual client since 1 January 1992.

Yours faithfully,

Tom Mackay — *Jonathan Bridger*
For Blake and Lander — *For Caspian Credit*

Mackay thought that, if the beauty of modern technology, in the form of electronic signatures, meant that he could tailor a standard audit bank letter and use the amended version to obtain unauthorised documents, then all was well and good with the information superhighway.

Surely it was a legitimate part of the audit anyway, he thought. Clearly the end justified the means, did it not? If he faxed this letter, was he betraying Bridger's trust? He might be. He certainly didn't have

Bridger's or Craven's authority to ask Avon and General for these documents, and it was probable that his actions would cause friction. In fact, what the hell was he doing? Had he forgotten that he didn't really give a shit?

He heard Sally coming out of her room and heading for the Ladies. It would be time to leave the office shortly, so he faxed the letter.

CHAPTER SEVEN

Wednesday 23 April 1997 – earlier the same day

Steadman got up, washed and began to shave, the procedure proving difficult because the mirror was still steamed up from Judith's earlier shower. He dressed and headed downstairs for breakfast, picking up a copy of The Times from reception on the way.

The young barman who had brought him his bar meal the previous night now acted as a waiter – Steadman knew that Judith had the morning off. He glanced at the waiter, who looked back at him with a sly smile. Steadman felt strangely embarrassed. How could this lad know about last night? The young man showed him to a seat with a view over the estuary and stood, ready to take his order.

'Full English please,' snapped Steadman. The waiter nodded and disappeared into the kitchen, where Steadman thought he could hear stifled laughter. He opened the paper and looked at the headlines.

MAJOR TAKES COMMAND FOR FINAL PUSH – *the battle switches to the cost of pensions.*

If it was a battle, thought Steadman, then it was largely an internal one, where the thin blue line had run out of ammo and been forced to bayonet rather than shoot each other, as Tony Blair and his New Labour hordes looked on, ready to mop up those Tories who were still standing. As in any apocalyptic defeat, there would of course be small groups of survivors, like Silas Craven. He'd only to turn up in Barnes and West Putney to get elected.

The thought of Craven reminded him of his appointment at Keepers Cottage. As it was approaching ten, he quickly finished his breakfast and left the Schooner. He'd passed the cottage on his way to the castle yesterday, so he easily retraced his steps and arrived punctually.

Like the Dower House, the cottage was of the same dressed ochre stone that the hall itself had been built with, and, also like the

Dower House, it probably formed part of the original estate. The garden easily lived up to the country cottage stereotype. Although small, it was crammed full of tiny stone paths, borders and hedges. Steadman was surprised at the jumbled mass of glorious colour so early in the season, with fuchsias and gladioli all jostling for space, light and the heat of the April sun.

He battled his way along a narrow path like some latter-day Chindit. A few seconds later, he was ambushed by Anne Gill, who'd been hiding behind some Oriental-looking bushes. She smiled broadly at him, shook his outstretched hand, and pivoted around to the front door, beckoning him to follow her.

'Please come in, Mr Steadman,' she said warmly. 'Do you want coffee? I take tea myself.'

'No. I mean yes. Tea will be fine, thank you.'

She showed him through to a sunroom, where he sat down in a comfortable old armchair. The room was glassed on three sides and south-east facing, with northerly views to the castle and southerly views over Alnmouth and its golf course.

He looked around the room and saw that Mrs Gill had all the *de rigueur* Miss Marple kit: plenty of lace doilies, bits and pieces of crockery and family pictures, including a wartime portrait of her husband in a RAF uniform, as well as all manner of useless-looking knick-knacks gathered over a long lifetime. If IKEA had arrived in England, it certainly hadn't reached Keeper's Cottage, Alnmouth.

She returned with a tray, complete with teapot and cosy, teacups, saucers and some heavy-looking scones weighed down with large dollops of butter and scoops of strawberry jam. Steadman felt a warm glow, and an alien sense of nationalism swept over him. He smiled at her as she sat down and began to pour the tea. If John Major's England of warm beer and old maidens cycling through village greens still existed anywhere, it was here, in rural Northumberland.

'I'm surprised that the garden has already come out,' he said, putting a third mouthful of scone into his mouth. The butter oozed between his teeth, just as it had done on his fried bread half an hour earlier. The thought of his fried breakfast and a second injection of cholesterol shortly afterwards unsettled him, and he felt the need to share his concern with Mrs Gill.

'Fried breakfast followed by buttered scones, Mrs Gill. I'm digging my grave with my knife and fork.'

'I've had butter all my life, Nick,' she replied genially, 'and look at me. I'm ninety next year.' She paused and looked out over the garden possessively. 'It's being by the coast, the garden I mean – we get a very temperate climate here.'

As if to evidence her assertion, the sun appeared from behind a cloud and seemed to concentrate all of its spring warmth directly into the sunroom, compelling Steadman to take off his jacket.

'Right. Silas Craven,' she said firmly, disturbing the tranquillity of the room. 'A crook and a murderer.'

CHAPTER EIGHT

Thursday 24 April 1997

KNIVES OUT FOR MAWHINNEY
IS HODDLE BEING DEVIOUS OR JUST PLAIN DAFT?
FRASER SHOULD WIN VOTE OVER SPIN DOCTORS

Mackay got up and felt seedy rather than hung-over. Despite plying Sally with several more gins and a half bottle of Jacob's Creek during supper, he'd got nowhere near enticing her back to his flat, though, surprisingly, she had agreed to go to Gibraltar - expenses paid - and share a room with him on a purely 'no sex basis.' In the cold light of day would she still come? If so, would the warm Mediterranean sun work to his advantage?

Instead of getting off the tube at Victoria, Mackay decided to go to Temple to see if there'd been a response from Avon and General. Predictably, Tony King was already in the office and moaning about the boxes stacked on his desk. Mackay noticed that he looked even duller than usual.

'Sorry, Tony, I'll get one of the juniors to move them.'

'You know that files are supposed to be in locked cabinets overnight, even in the office,' said King.

'Well, it was pretty late,' replied Mackay defensively, with a huge evidential yawn. Simply talking to King made him feel tired: he was like a bespectacled parasite, drawing energy from his hosts, then chewing it up and spitting it out in large dollops of audit waste.

As their shared fax was empty, and there was nothing in his pigeonhole except a technical brief about FRS 7, 'Fair values in acquisition accounting', which went straight in the bin, Mackay left the room and headed for the juniors area. As Kyle Jones wasn't there, he called into the secretaries' room, where he found the Welshman flirting with Erica Quirke.

'I'm glad I've caught you both,' began Mackay. 'Have either of you moved or sent any of Keith's boxes back to archives in the last few days, from that Caspian audit he was doing?' They both shook their heads.

'Could have been Julie though,' said Erica. 'She sent something down the other day, but she's off sick again. I had a look for the archive records yesterday but I couldn't find them. Jules must have put them somewhere.'

'Can we call her?' asked Mackay, frustrated that the system should collapse because of the absence of the junior secretary.

Erica looked panicked. 'I've tried her on her landline and mobile already. She must have been asleep.'

Mackay sensed that Julie's sick day might be integral to a long weekend spent somewhere nice, and that Erica had been asked to cover for her. Having done the same himself on a number of occasions, he didn't press any further.

'Well if you *do* manage to get hold of her, put her through to me at Caspian,' he said with a knowing smile. Erica got the message and looked relieved. Mackay turned slightly to face Jones. 'Kyle, did Keith ever mention a large insurance rebate when you were out there with him?'

'No, boss,' he replied sarcastically. 'We only crossed over for half a day, said he would prefer to do a cold review rather than have me hanging around. Made no mention of any rebate.'

Mackay thought for a moment. 'You sure he always left the key to the audit cupboard on the right of the flipchart?'

'Every time,' replied Jones. He hesitated and a unique look of seriousness crossed his face. 'You think someone's been messing with the audit files?'

'Maybe.' Mackay turned to leave then glanced back at Jones. 'Do us a favour and send the boxes in my room back to archives. They're annoying Wan, who's annoying me.'

'Will do,' said the Welshman.

Mackay left the room and set off for Connaught Lane. He arrived half an hour later. He unlocked the audit cupboard and put the files on the boardroom table. He could see Jonathan Bridger wasn't in his office and that Mrs Paterson wasn't at her desk.

Other than the insurance issue and a discussion about the provisioning levels, the audit was more or less finished. As Caspian had only made £15 million this year, some of the provisions would have to be released and the net profit figure fudged, just as it had been every year for the last six years, but there was no way Craven could ignore the insurance rebate. £7 million was too big to be kicked into next year

There was a knock at the glass door and two men walked in uninvited. Mackay knew instantly they were policemen. The shorter of the two men was the most senior. He was Teutonic looking with fairly long blond hair, blue eyes and a clean-cut angular jaw. He could have been thirty or forty – it was difficult to tell, as he had a Peter Pan-like quality to him.

'I'm Detective Inspector Woodhouse,' he said, 'and this is Detective Sergeant Thorpe. Would you mind if we asked you a few questions?' Mackay had seen countless police dramas and had always wondered whether policemen introduced themselves the way they did on the telly – perhaps it was standard police procedure.

'Of course, please sit down.' They sat down and the sergeant took out a black leather notebook. 'Any closer to tracking down the hit-and-run driver?' asked Mackay.

The senior policeman smiled, ignored his question, and then asked his own. 'You've taken over where Mr Platt left off then, Tom. Anything unusual you've noticed?'

Mackay wanted to run the insurance query past Craven first. His theories on missing audit schedules, re-archived boxes and tampered audit files were pure speculation. Mackay might look foolish if he told the police about them now without having any hard evidence. Unfortunately, this briefest of hesitations was picked up by the policemen.

'No, nothing at all.' They looked disbelievingly at him and he quickly added, 'but I haven't finished the audit yet.'

There was a long pause as the inspector examined Mackay more closely. Mackay had very dark brown hair, almost black, which was curly in places and falling haphazardly over his brown eyes. The focal point of his face was his toothy grin, which, when combined with his dark skin and swarthy looks, hinted at a touch of Irish or even Romany ancestry. He was of average height and stocky build. His suit was smart enough but definitely off the peg, probably Moss Bros or the Savoy Tailors Guild, and his shirt was poorly ironed and undone at the collar. He looked untrustworthy and he had dithered at the first question. He might know something.

'Did you know Mr Platt well, sir,' said the inspector, hissing the last word and stripping it of any element of deference or politeness.

'Not really. We knew each other through work - we were colleagues rather than friends. Do you think that his death might not have been accidental?'

'No, we're treating it as a hit-and-run at this stage,' said the sergeant. 'We have to investigate all possibilities though, you understand.'

'Of course,' said Mackay.

The inspector handed Mackay a card. 'Well, if anything odd should come up during your work, please call me on this number.'

The policemen got up and headed for the door, where the inspector turned and looked at the seated auditor, who fidgeted in anticipation of an incoming Columbo-style killer question. Instead, the policeman simply said, 'anything out of the ordinary or trivial looking, you let me know.'

'I will,' lied Mackay

CHAPTER NINE

Friday 25 April 1997

THE ECONOMIST BACKS MAJOR
COMPUTER GEEKS BURST INTO BLOOM
BARCLAYS BUOYANT ON BZW RUMOURS

Mackay was surprised there'd been no sign of Bridger during the day and that Craven hadn't phoned. A quick call to the office established that Craven's secretary Sarah didn't know where Craven was, and a word with Mrs Paterson determined that Bridger had also disappeared. Plus, no fax had arrived from Avon and General.

All in all, it was a quiet day, and Mackay didn't feel like he was at the centre of a massive fraud perpetrated on Southern and London shareholders. He'd spoken to Sally at lunchtime to tell her he'd booked her Gibraltar flight, and she had told him to stop imagining things. The more he thought about it, the more he became convinced that she was right. Platt had been killed by a hit-and-run driver, there was no £7 million pound rebate, and Julie had archived the Caspian files after Platt's death.

As was usual for him on a Friday, he decided to knock off early. He threw the audit files and his briefcase into the cupboard and locked it, then took off his jacket and tie, opened his holdall, and took out his jeans. He returned from the third-floor toilet five minutes later, transformed from City auditor to determined Sally Purcell pursuer.

He knew the Caspian staff were gossiping about his early departure when he left, and he knew it wasn't very professional behaviour, but he didn't care. A weekend in the sun, expenses paid – a weekend without Commander Roper and the Cresswell Estate, and a weekend spent with Sally Purcell. What could be more perfect? The only downside was leaving Annabel to a predatory Craven.

Mackay walked to Victoria. He wasn't due to meet Sally at the Gatwick Express until 4pm so he went into Coopers bar for a pint. He ordered a ropey-looking bitter and sat down on one of the bar stools closest to the door.

From where he was sitting, he had a clear view of the concourse in front of him and the busy tube exit to his right. The concourse was already packed with fellow travellers, who, like Mackay, had knocked off early to beat the weekend rush, except that, like most Fridays, because a large number of commuters had the same idea, there was very little beating going on and a lot of rushing.

Mackay saw the platform number for the Brighton train called. The stationary 'mass' that had formed in front of the departure board took on a new shape. The 'mass' now lived and breathed, its behaviour erratic, unpredictable and, above all, selfish. While the original semi-circular shape of the 'mass' was maintained in skeleton form by the non-Brighton commuters, the bulk of it moved slowly towards the narrow gap leading onto the platform.

Clearly oblivious to the huge 'mass' rumbling past them, the 'revenue protection officials' who'd been idling about the Costa Coffee kiosk moments before decided to carry out a ticket inspection. This necessitated closing one of the two gates that guarded the gap and meant that the speed at which the 'mass' was travelling was more than halved, with the effect of bringing out the most selfish characteristics of the 'mass'. The area in front of the gap degenerated into a melee.

Mackay chuckled to himself. Other than blood sports, which was a rural activity, there was nowhere urban in a Western democracy he'd rather be to witness the primeval nature of man than at Victoria station.

Mackay was distracted from his zoological observations by a man he recognised walking out of the tube exit to his right. It was the journalist he'd met the previous weekend. Mackay knocked on the window and Steadman spun round. The journalist scanned the windows of the bar, saw Mackay, half-waved, stood motionless for a moment, then, deciding to join him, headed inside.

'Hi, good to see you, Tom,' said Steadman. 'Can I get you a pint?'

'A quick one, thanks. I'm catching the Gatwick Express at four. In fact, I'd better have a short – make it a gin and tonic.'

Steadman went to the bar and returned with two large G&Ts. 'Off somewhere nice for the weekend?' he asked.

Mackay sipped his drink. 'Gibraltar. My uncle died the other day and I'm an executor of his estate. Got some paperwork to sort out.' Mackay saw Steadman become animated at the mention of Gibraltar.

'Gibraltar! I can't believe it – what a coincidence.'

'What is?' said Mackay eagerly, blindly sharing the journalist's enthusiasm.

Steadman was excited. 'You're going to Gibraltar. Listen, I don't mind admitting that I've been up north for the last few days checking on the background of your boss. I just arrived back at King's Cross half an hour ago. What I've heard, if true, is pretty disturbing. I'd watch out for him if I were you. Er…sorry to hear about your uncle by the way.'

'You mean Silas Craven?' said Mackay, ignoring the heartfelt condolences.

'Yes. I don't have any hard evidence, but you can help me get it.'

Mackay's concerns about Craven and the Caspian job were beginning to solidify. 'What's he supposed to have done?'

Steadman gulped down his spirits. 'Serious stuff, but if you don't mind I've got to check one or two things out first. I don't want to slander him, do I? You saw how litigious he might be. But you can help, simply by checking something out at the local paper in Gib.'

'Give us an idea,' said an intrigued Mackay, worried that his conspiracy theories were on the point of being irreversibly revived.

'All I'll say is that it involves criminal allegations, but I must qualify that and say again that I've no hard evidence.'

'Bloody hell,' said Mackay, thinking of Platt's death. He was tempted to mention it to Steadman but decided against it. 'Look, tell me what to look for, and if I do find anything out, I'll let you know, if you agree to tell me what the allegations are first.'

'Fine,' said the journalist, pulling a green hardback notebook from his overnight bag.

Mackay saw that the notebook had the Borough Gazette emblazoned in silver on the top right-hand cover.

'It's all in here,' Steadman was saying. 'If this is true, it'll be this administration's final scandal.'

'He's not even an MP yet,' said Mackay. 'It'll make no difference to the overall result.'

'No,' replied Steadman, 'but it'll mean the voters of Barnes and West Putney don't elect a crook.'

Steadman continued to flick through the pages of the notebook and Mackay noticed that he'd inked 'NJS' under the Gazette's lettering on the front cover: Nick J. Steadman, he thought.

'Here it is,' said Steadman. 'Christ, I can never read my own writing. I guess being a journalist I should improve my shorthand. OK, yes, this is what she said. Craven was involved with a company called the Gibraltar and Atlantic General Trading Company. My information is that it went bust in early 1976 and Craven cooked the books for it, or at least was mixed up in it. Not much to go on I know, but a warmish lead.'

Mackay jotted down the company name in his Blake and Lander diary and finished his drink. 'No promises Nick, this won't be top of my agenda this weekend.'

Steadman followed Mackay's gaze to platform eleven, where a shapely, attractive girl, with discreetly highlighted and loosely bobbed hair stood waving at them.

'I see,' said Steadman, with an understanding smile. 'Well, enjoy yourself, and…er…good luck.'

'Thanks,' said Mackay, getting up to leave. 'I will.'

Mackay skirted around the 'mass' and joined Sally on platform eleven. She looked even better from a few feet away. She gave him a friendly peck on the cheek and dived into the nearest carriage, which they soon discovered, was almost empty.

Alighting on the Gatwick Express was always more civilised than boarding the standard service trains. This was not only because of the emptier carriages, but also because of the non-stop, more frequent service - a glance at the tickets reminded Mackay that the hike in the fare might also have something to do with it.

'Who were you speaking to in the bar?' asked Sally, as the train sped through Clapham Junction.

'A journalist I met at a Tory Party thing last weekend – Nick Steadman, nice chap. He's doing pen portraits of the candidates in my constituency.' He paused. 'Did you know Silas Craven is the Tory candidate?'

'Yes, I'd heard that. Will he be elected?'

'Yep, it's the sort of constituency where a hat stand wearing a blue rosette gets elected.'

She looked at him. 'I'm surprised you're involved with politics. I never had you marked down as an activist.'

He laughed. 'Unlike you, you mean. I remember you're a big Clinton fan. You must be happy with last November and Bill's big win.'

'I am, although I remain concerned about his roving eye. I met him a few times during the '92 campaign and felt he was undressing me with his eyes.'

Mackay looked closely at Sally and didn't find the president's actions surprising. 'Yes, he comes across as that type. I bet he's played away.'

'You really think so? It wouldn't surprise me.' An image of the Oval Office and the Resolution desk crossed her mind. 'I just can see there being an opportunity given the confines of the White House.'

'To go back to your question, Sal, no, I'm not really political. I suppose I'm a fan of Major – the Brixton boy made good bit does impress me. I just feel he's been badly let down by those dozen twats in his own party who had the whip withdrawn. A majority of twenty-one was never enough to start with, even without ten of your own team playing offside.'

He paused to think. 'Who'll have heard of Eurosceptics like George Gardiner, Theresa Gorman and Richard Body in a few years' time? Nobody, but the damage those muppets have done will keep the Tories out of office for at least three terms.'

'You see, you care more than you think. Are you pro-European yourself?'

'I don't really care whether I buy my pint with a pound or a euro – it's just a name. As long as it means we all get richer – as Europeans I mean. It has to be more sensible being able to take my ten euros out of a cash machine at Victoria and spend the same ten euros in Spain, France or Greece. It's more efficient, plus it's all done without the involvement of a foreign exchange dealer in the City. I hate the way the commission I pay enables those bastards to buy red Ferraris.' He paused. 'My only concern is that conceptually it has to ultimately lead to a single European state, can't see a way round it, and I don't want that.'

'I think you'll find a federal system works very well,' she said, teasing him. 'Look across the pond or at Australia.'

He smiled. 'I take your point with Australia but let's leave an argument about the US for another day. Look, we've a lot to learn from the Europeans and they've a lot to learn from us. I'm not saying that there aren't problems – there are huge problems, like the bloated public sectors and high taxation they have on the Continent, the common agricultural policy, outdated industrial practices. Christ, the French are on strike every other week – their lorry drivers blocking every road in France. We got rid of all that crap during the eighties and we don't want it reintroduced here, via Brussels. We can teach them how to govern themselves better.'

'That's quite a tirade, Tom, though if I could vote here, you'd still not get me to vote Tory. Five years of more or less continuous sleaze

– you can't defend that.' She was deliberately provoking him and he liked it.

He laughed. 'I'm astonished the media has penetrated your cynicism shield, Sal. This sleaze brush the government's been tarred with, it's all sexual. Neil Hamilton got, what, two grand in a brown envelope – the Continentals wouldn't get out of bed for a bung that size. This country has less corruption than anywhere else in the world.' He paused. 'Do you know what baksheesh is?'

The word reminded her of a travel guide and a holiday in Egypt but she couldn't remember what it was. 'I've heard of it,' she said neutrally.

'Well it's a term for institutionalised bribery – it goes on just about everywhere else in the world except on this island, and, as for sexual impropriety, who gives a shit? It doesn't affect the performance of the government.'

'Actually, it does make a difference Tom,' she said, 'especially when the government makes a point of trumpeting family values.'

He paused and thought of the prime minister and old maids bicycling through the morning mist. 'Yes, you're probably right there. I'm pretty sure Major regrets having made that Back to Basics speech. I reiterate what I said earlier, though – he's been let down by his ministers, but he's pretty sleaze free himself.'

'I wouldn't bet on that,' she said. 'It's always the quiet ones that surprise you. There's a certain ethereal sexuality about him – it's his smile that does it. It makes you want to cuddle him. I can see some women going for him in a big way, even without the power thing.'

'Really?' said Mackay, intrigued by her insight. 'You think he might have strayed away?'

'Yep.'

Mackay considered the suspects. 'Who? Virginia Bottomley? That's what they thought on *Spitting Image*.'

Sally paused to think. 'No, I can't see it. Besides, her husband's an MP as well, isn't he? Difficult to see how they would get an opportunity.'

'Who else is there? There aren't many women in the cabinet.' He searched his memory to find one. 'Gillian Shepherd?'

'She's employment secretary, isn't she?' asked Sally. 'I always get her confused with Edwina Currie.'

'They do look pretty similar,' agreed Mackay, remembering the Queen of Salmonella. 'No, I doubt it. I think your theory's bollocks. I just can't see 'Honest John' straying from the home patch.'

They arrived at the airport forty minutes later. Mackay was surprised how busy it was. Like the rail commuters at Victoria station, the airport travellers exhibited 'mass-like' characteristics, except that the airport 'mass' was structured into chunky gridlines emanating from the check-in desks rather than the loose semi-circle that had formed under Victoria's departure board.

'Where are all these people going?' asked Sally, semi-rhetorically, as they joined the check-in queue.

'Don't know,' replied Mackay. 'Some of them look well heeled though, and they've got a lot of stuff with them. I guess they must be fleeing the capital – the Reds are at the gate you know.'

Mackay wasn't convinced there were many parallels between Saigon in April 1975 and Gatwick in April 1997, though he suspected most Daily Mail readers didn't understand the difference between the Vietcong and New Labour. Nevertheless, he was pleased to hear Sally laughing quietly to herself, sharing the weak joke.

'Yes,' she said. 'I think Tony Blair would look great in a huge red neckerchief sitting astride a tank rumbling into Parliament Square.'

Mackay smiled at her. 'With a guitar on his back of course.'

'Naturally.'

They checked in but were delayed for a few minutes at passport control while an officer checked Sally's visa. Once they were through, she turned to Mackay, the irritation clear in her voice. 'He was a bit fussy, wasn't he?'

'Was he? I thought he was pretty quick.' Mackay paused. 'I guess you haven't been through US border control as a foreigner. Some of your guys are just plain awkward.'

She didn't reply and they went through security and into Departures.

'Don't bother getting any duty free here, Sal. I remember my uncle saying it's cheaper in Gib.'

'OK, but I fancy doing some window shopping;' she said, scanning the rest of the lounge. She turned to face him. 'I'll meet you in that bar over there in half an hour.' He acknowledged her instructions with a nod of his head and headed towards the bar.

The BA flight to Gibraltar took just under three hours. As Mackay had expected, the closer they got to Spain, the more the cloud thinned. He reflected that, if he'd been in a science lab and had the tools to plot accurately, he felt sure he could have laid claim to some new principle of meteorology, Mackay's Law perhaps, as there seemed to be an exact correlation between the miles travelled southwards towards their destination and the reduced cloud density. By the time they approached The Rock itself, although it was getting dark, Mackay could see that the sky was cloudless.

The plane approached the territory from the west, and, as Mackay had a window seat on the starboard side of the cabin, he was well sighted to see the enormous hunk of limestone jutting half a kilometre out of the southerly tip of Europe.

When the plane then banked to the right, the strip of silvery lights shining from the main town at the bottom of the Rock and further bright lights at its southerly point gave the Rock the appearance of an enormous steel toe-capped boot, a Dr Martin perhaps, guarding the Straits of Gibraltar and kicking unwelcome visitors straight back into the Atlantic.

Mackay could see that the five-kilometre-long Rock was sandwiched between the Bay of Algeciras to the west and the Mediterranean to the east, and, because of the narrow isthmus connecting it to Spain, it looked very much like an island.

Landing on runways partially reclaimed from the sea was always more exciting than coming down on conventional runways, and Gibraltar was no different. When they touched down, Mackay was all too aware of seawater a few feet to his right, a few feet to his left, and just ahead of him.

As the pilot wrestled with the brakes and the plane unresponsively sped closer to the Med, Mackay furtively stole a glance at the nearest emergency exit and was sorely tempted to grab hold of Sally's hand. Not because his own nerves needed steadying, but because comforting a young lady who was likely to be in distress was the gentlemanly thing to do.

'Must be a fairly tight landing this,' she said, with self-assured fragility.

The opportunity was too good to miss, and he slipped her hand inside his and held it tightly. He was pleased when she waited for the plane to come to a standstill before withdrawing it.

As they got off the plane, the warm air, even at that time of night, indicated that summer had already started in Gibraltar. Caspian, Bridger, Craven, Steadman, conspiracy theories, the joys of London and the beleaguered Tories - they were all a long way away, replaced instead by the delights of Sally Purcell.

They passed through customs and passport control quickly, and took a taxi to The Rock Hotel. It soon became apparent that their route skirted the main town, so the travellers had to make do with brief glimpses of Marks and Spencer, red post boxes, soldiers in white pith helmets and other such signs of Britishness for which the Rock was famous.

The hotel drive was extremely steep, making it difficult to see what the hotel looked like as they approached it. Mackay had expected a period building with airy verandas and an atmosphere similar to the gentlemen's clubs he'd visited in London. Instead, the modern-looking building was of the white cubicle type, typical of the early Costa Blanca style.

They got out of the taxi, went into the building and checked in. It was comfortable enough inside, but, after they'd entered their room and opened the shutters onto their balcony, the principal strength of the hotel became apparent. Even in the half-light, they could see that the views over the bay to Spain and across the Straits of Gibraltar to Morocco and the Atlas mountains were stunning.

'This is great,' said Sally. 'Let's leave the unpacking and head down for dinner. It's already late.'

They both ordered fish. Their starters arrived a few minutes later. 'Is this a fast food restaurant?' joked Sally.

Mackay saw that most of their fellow diners were nearing the end of their meals. He observed that they had two waiters all to themselves and the entire kitchen staff devoted to the preparation of their food. He felt that they were in danger of finishing too quickly – more importantly, before he'd an opportunity to order a second bottle of wine.

There was still a third of the first bottle left when the fish arrived, so he took a large gulp out of his own glass, refilled it and crammed as much as could into Sally's glass, merging the meniscus and top of the glass into one.

She took a sip, but the glass was too full, and wine dribbled enticingly down her chin. 'Are you trying to get me pissed?' she said with a smile.

'Course not,' lied Mackay. 'Shall we have another bottle though?' He could see from her face that he'd been premature – perhaps he shouldn't have consulted her and just ordered it anyway. Either way, it was too late.

'I think this one will do, Tom. I've plenty here.'

Mackay began to nurse his own drink, resigned to the fact that his quest wouldn't be aided by the second bottle. Unbeknown to him, though, help was on hand from an unexpected quarter.

The restaurant was empty except for a group of elderly Germans, who had massed at the best tables nearest to the windows. The largest of these Germans, clean shaven, balding, very fat and wearing a loose-fitting blue shirt in the Hawaiian style, was Klaus.

Mackay knew his name was Klaus because, a few minutes earlier, the head waiter had arrived at Klaus's table with a large birthday cake, and a chorus of Happy Birthday, in English, had soon followed. It turned out that Klaus was eighty, and, if the dozen or so Germans had been boisterous before the arrival of the cake and their spirited rendition of Happy Birthday, they were positively noisy afterwards.

Klaus had schnapps with his wife, schnapps with his fellow Germans, schnapps with the head waiter, schnapps with the other waiters, and the chef, who had no doubt baked the cake, was summoned from the kitchen and given schnapps. Finally, just as Mackay was finishing his glass of wine, he became aware of a large blue Hawaiian shirt heading in his direction.

'You will have some schnapps with me,' said the German, looking at Sally.

'Yes, of course I will,' replied the American, gulping down the remainder of her wine.

Klaus tipped the bottle upside down and the schnapps splashed freely into their empty glasses, filling them halfway.

'To you, Klaus,' she said, raising her glass. 'Happy birthday.'

'Down in one, after three,' insisted the octogenarian German, filling up his own thimble-sized schnapps glass. 'One, two, three.'

They downed their drinks simultaneously. Unused to the burning liquid, Sally gasped and Mackay stifled a girly cough. 'Bloody hell,' he gasped. 'Happy birthday, Klaus.'

'Cheers,' said the beaming German, who turned slowly round like a steam train on a turntable before heading back to his friends.

'Well, I'm up for a party now, Tom,' said the flushed American. 'You Europeans have given me a bit of a buzz. Shall we get another bottle, or do you fancy heading out?'

'Let's skip dessert and head into town.'

'OK,' she replied, putting her napkin on the table. 'Let's go.'

Mackay stood up. The beauty of full board, he reflected, was that you simply left when you'd finished eating. There was no need to catch the waiter's eye, ask for the bill, hang around for ten minutes while he found it, then, after you'd checked it and attached your card to it, catch his eye again and wait a further ten minutes for him to put it through the machine. He liked full board.

They walked through reception and down the hotel's steep drive. A few minutes later, they were in the Gibraltar Arms on Main Street.

They talked and drank, and drank and talked, until they were both drunk. It was after midnight when Sally noticed the pub was empty and the barman had put the stools on top of the bar.

'I feel like your mistress, Tom,' she drawled. 'Expenses-paid weekend in the sun, great hotel, great food, loads of booze. Still waiting for the expensive jewellery, though.' She paused. 'And not a single thought of my deceased boyfriend.'

'Let's face it, he was pretty bloody dull,' slurred Mackay.

There was a long silence as they both thought of Platt.

Mackay spoke first. 'Getting back to the mistress bit,' he said, with a dirty smile.

'What of it?' she replied, with faked innocence.

'Being a mistress brings with it…er… certain obligations, as well as the benefits you just mentioned.'

'What obligations might they be, kind sir?' she said mischievously, fluttering her eyelids like a Southern belle.

'Sexual obligations,' he said firmly. They looked at each other and he reached forwards and kissed her.

She responded, but pulled back when the impatient barman deliberately clattered some chairs. 'Well, if it's my duty as a mistress,' she said, with mock resentment, swaying slightly as she got to her feet, 'we'd better get on with it.'

'Bloody hell,' said Mackay, for the second time that evening, leaping from his chair.

The journey back to the hotel seemed all too long and the hotel drive all too steep, as the lusty number crunchers staggered, lurched and giggled their way back to their hotel room. When they got there, Mackay lay on the bed alone, concerned he might have had *too* much to drink and that this might lead to a devastating physical problem. However, the sight of Sally bolting naked from behind the bathroom door soon demonstrated that these fears were unwarranted.

Mackay wasn't sure what or where nirvana was, but he knew that that sunny Saturday in Gibraltar got pretty close to it. To begin with, the happy bean counters took the cable car to the top of the Rock and flirted publicly while enjoying the views. Then they showed a flagrant disregard for the regulations and fed the Barbary Apes. They visited St Michael's Cave and talked loudly during a guided tour, before playing at Spanish invaders and British defenders in the O'Hara battery. Finally, when they couldn't hold on any longer, they skipped down the Mediterranean Steps back to their hotel room and spent the rest of the afternoon and early evening in bed.

'What a lovely day, Tom,' said Sally, yawning. It had been an active day.

'Yes, cracking day, Sal. Same again tomorrow?' he said, flicking through a newly acquired guidebook and only half hearing her. 'Interesting what that tour guide at St Michael's Cave said today, I mean about Gibraltar's history. I always thought the reason folk on this Rock didn't want to hook up with Spain was because they know how good they've got it here – low taxes, virtually duty-free goods, plus having the UK's muscle when you need it – it's a good deal. They had a valid argument twenty odd years ago, and, although I claim to be right of centre politically, I wouldn't have fancied living in Franco's Spain. Now, though, it's different.'

She looked at him with a half-frown. 'You've confused me. Are you saying they should be joined back up with Spain or not?'

'Not. It's the historical context, you see. They don't feel any more Spanish than you or I do. It was like that guide was saying today in the cave. Up until…when was it…' Mackay consulted his guidebook. '1462, the Rock was controlled by the Moors and over there wasn't even called Spain. The Moors called it al-Andalus, so when the British arrived in 1713 the Spanish had only been here her for about 250 years, whereas the British have now been here for nearly 300 years already. Plus the Spanish still have their own enclaves in Morocco. What did he say they were called? Ceuta, and something.'

'Melilla, I think it was.'

Mackay paused to think. 'No wonder folk here are a bit concerned about Thursday. Can't see the wishes of 30,000 Gibraltarians cutting much ice in Milbank, even if they did help us in our hour of greatest need.'

'No,' said Sally thoughtfully. 'Colony and imperial aren't words you're likely to find in New Labour jargon. But I do think they'll be in for a shock when their ethical foreign policy, whatever that means, hits reality.' She rolled over to his side of the bed and ran her hands through his hair. 'You think you don't care, but you're more of a political animal than you realise.' She paused. 'But we've had nothing but politics for the last month and I'm sick of it. Give me that guide, and *I'll* decide what we're doing tomorrow.'

Their Sunday was much the same as their Saturday, except that the sights were different. First, they visited the Moorish castle and its keep – the Tower of Homage, then the spectacular fourteenth-century Moorish baths, which were incorporated into the Gibraltar museum. On their way to Europa Point, the most southerly point on the European mainland, they stopped off at Trafalgar Cemetery, where those who had survived the French and the Spanish were brought onshore to be killed off by Royal Navy surgeons.

'Look at this one, Sal,' said Mackay, pointing to one of the few readable headstones. *'Lieutenant, William Forster, late of his Majesty's Ship Colossus, died of the wounds he received in the glorious Battle of Trafalgar, the 21 day of October 1805, aged 20.'*

'Poor lad,' said Sally. 'I bet "died of his wounds" covers all manner of medical incompetence and unsanitary conditions.'

They continued on foot for half an hour in a southerly direction, passing the naval base, commercial docks and a series of decaying Second World War military buildings.

'It's in a bit of a time warp, this place,' said Mackay, as they passed a dilapidated green building, which looked like it might have been a hospital. 'I'm surprised the Tories haven't tried to sell some of this off – there's a lot of empty real estate here.'

Sally halted to look into the complex. 'Maybe NATO has told them to hang on to it and the MOD is getting a bung for doing so.'

'By NATO, you mean your generals?' said Mackay.

She smiled at him. 'Yes, NATO, the US military. To me they're the same thing.'

He laughed. 'We are after all the fifty-first state.'

They reached Europa Point, sweating profusely. Mackay regretted not having a hat and Sally regretted the lack of a water bottle. They both regretted walking for an hour in the blazing midday sun.

Looking out across the Straits, Mackay noted from his guidebook that there'd been a naval base in Gibraltar since Phoenician times. He could see why. The strategic importance of the Rock was obvious. Any unwelcome shipping passing through this gateway to the Mediterranean could be shelled, either by warships or by the batteries behind him. He saw now why, in the age of sea power, the Rock had been in the hands of the Royal Navy for 300 years.

'Well, here we are, Sal,' said Mackay, clumsily putting his arm around her in an attempt to create a romantic moment. 'The Continent doesn't go any further south. We're at the end of Europe.'

'Thought you said somewhere in Spain is further south?'

'Don't spoil the moment with facts please, Sal,' he said with mock irritation.

'She's right, young fella,' came a loud American voice from behind them. 'There's a place called Tarifa over there on the Spanish mainland, which is further south.'

Mackay looked around and saw that the voice of the slayer of romantic moments fitted the stereotype. The man was close to crossing the boundary between very fat and obese. He wore a white linen shirt, which was somehow tucked into his beige tailored shorts. On his head, he wore the obligatory white baseball cap with 'US' splashed in large red letters on the front, just in case he forgot his own nationality.

Mackay glanced at Sally, who smiled first at Mackay then at her countryman. Mackay was slightly irritated, and continued, 'we can all agree this isn't the most southerly point of Europe then.'

'You're welcome' said the American cheerily. 'Where you from?' he asked Sally.

'Washington,' she replied.

'I'm from Richmond, Virginia. Been over in Europe for…' The noise of an engine cut him off and they looked over to the road.

Mackay was relieved. 'That's our bus, Sal. Nice to have met you,' he said.

'Likewise,' said the man.

As they boarded the bus, the helpful American passed them, waving, in a huge rented Range Rover.

CHAPTER TEN

Monday 28 April 1997

TORY BIG GUNS TURN ON CURRIE
ST TRINIAN'S TO RETURN WITH SPICE GIRL POWER
GOLDEN YEARS COME FLOODING BACK AS ARMS PARK PREPARES FOR BULLDOZERS

The firm of Likudi, Benady, Gomez and Scott Solicitors was located on Linewall Road, which Mackay found without difficulty the following day. He saw that all the buildings on Linewall Road were old, and the building belonging to the legal representatives of his deceased uncle was no exception. The Georgian structure had three storeys and had the obligatory brass plaque with the partners' names inscribed on it. He noticed that the first name on the plaque was John Benady, Mr Likudi presumably having reached the lucrative, yet undemanding, semi-retired role of consultant.

The entrance to number 8B Linewall Road was through a set of large blue double doors, with the '8' on the left-hand door and the 'B' on the right. Mackay discovered that only the right-hand door opened. He went inside and was shown to a waiting room. The look, feel and atmosphere of the office felt like that of an expanding provincial legal practice in the Home Counties, but it wasn't – it wasn't quite English.

At nine o'clock he was shown into the room of the senior partner, who sat behind a mahogany desk with a green leather inlay. Mackay saw all manner of weighty legal tomes, digests and law reports crammed onto every shelf in the room, each book no doubt very important, written in that legal speak that lawyers are at pains to ensure no layman can understand.

Like his offices, John Benady was English but somehow not English. English was obviously his native tongue, but the way he spoke, his accent, the words he used, weren't quite English. He didn't look

English, but then again he didn't look Spanish. His skin was dark, darker than Mackay's, but his eyes were bright blue, almost Nordic looking.

'I trust you're enjoying your stay on the Rock,' he said smoothly, after their introductions. 'Did you bring your wife with you?'

'Yes, well my…er…girlfriend actually. I've sent her to Main Street to get some duty free.' Was she his girlfriend? He liked the idea of it but suspected she wouldn't see things in the same way.

The solicitor pulled open a drawer on his desk and handed him a card. 'If you wish to purchase duty free, I suggest you try here - your goods will cost half the price of Main Street. Main Street is just for the…'He paused, deliberating carefully over his next word, '…tourists. Please mention my name to the proprietor and you may get an additional discount.'

'Thanks very much,' said Mackay.

'Don't mention it. I was very fond of your uncle. I spent many a long evening with him at his villa, and, as a consequence, I'll always associate mornings there with a sore head.' He paused, and Mackay sensed that he was smiling internally. 'And now to business. Your uncle was a man of some estate.'

The accountant and the lawyer spent the morning poring over the will, probate documents and assets and liabilities. By lunchtime, Mackay began to feel that the trip had begun to look like a busman's holiday, and he was concerned at how his uncle's liabilities had mounted up, from mortgages and undischarged bank loans to unpaid grocery and utility bills - all in all, his creditors were owed over £500,000, but the assets were larger.

Mackay had hoped there might be some way that he and his sister could hang on to his uncle's villa - a light, spacious, beautifully converted former water mill in Jimenez de la Frontera, a mountain village about twenty miles inland. However, as the principal asset, valued at over £1 million, this had proved unrealistic, especially as he guessed that his cousins had no interest in it and would prefer the cash.

There was also a small flat in St John's Wood, and the balance was made up of cash, government bonds and equities.

Benady was also in favour of retaining the villa in Jimenez, but for different reasons. 'Of course, your uncle never fully disclosed all of his financial affairs to me,' he began, with a lawyer's usual disclaimer of liability, 'but I couldn't swear to the fact that all the money your uncle used to purchase the villa, was...er...taxed.'

Benady paused to study Mackay's reaction, which seemed to pass the test, because he continued in the same vein as before. 'Also, given that your uncle wasn't tax resident in the UK, and that he hadn't lived in the UK for some years, one might argue that he'd lost his UK domesticity for inheritance tax purposes. On that basis, and considering that the property *is* in Spain, it might be reasonably argued that the villa, for the Inland Revenue's purposes, shouldn't form part of his estate. In fact, perhaps there's no need to disclose the existence of the villa to the Revenue at all.'

Benady stopped and looked closely at Mackay again, who looked back at him with a blank expression. Mackay had failed his tax exams on several occasions and, when he'd eventually passed them, it would have been fair *then* to describe his tax knowledge as patchy. Now he simply knew nothing, except that he did remember that the golden rule was that you never hid anything from the taxman, and that those who did had something to hide and did so at their own peril.

'But wouldn't the villa have to be somehow taxed in Spain?' asked Mackay neutrally. He wasn't really interested in the solicitor's response. It was clear to him that after his uncle's business – Sharp's Motors – had been sold, Benady had in some way helped his uncle bring some, if not all, of the untaxed proceeds into Spain. Knowing his uncle, this would probably have involved suitcases full of cash. Whatever the method was, it was plain that Benady felt a little exposed.

'Yes, maybe a little tax,' said Benady, encouraged by Mackay's question, 'but it's easier to make it disappear over here, where there are more loopholes and grey areas.'

Mackay was a professional, and professionals didn't defraud the Revenue, not illegally anyway. Of course, he knew that the partners at Blake and Lander paid less tax than a bin man, but the advantage of having the best tax advice was that there were all manner of legal dodges, tricks and avoidance measures that could be employed to avoid a liability.

Mackay knew that it would be to his personal benefit to hide the villa from the Revenue, and if it could be done by bending the rules then he would have been up for it, but there was a difference between bending and breaking, and this sounded like breaking. At the moment, though, he was keen to keep the solicitor on side, and his instinct told him not to knock back the lawyer's help - not at this stage anyway.

'Sounds like it should be something to consider, John,' Mackay said collaboratively. 'Let me think about it over the next few days.'

'Good idea,' said Benady enthusiastically, certain that Mackay had adopted his scheme. 'Even if we don't go ahead with this, I suggest that you set up a personal bank account here in Gibraltar. There may be some other bits and pieces that can be usefully kept offshore and remitted back to the UK at your leisure, depending on your own tax circumstances in any one particular year. I can sort this out within a day or two - I tend to use the Gibraltar and West Mediterranean Bank, or the GWM as we call it. I have the forms here if you'd care to sign them now.'

Mackay signed the forms and handed them back to the solicitor. 'Well, that's about everything. I'll be in touch during the week to finalise our options.'

'There's one other thing, John.'

'What is it?'

'A friend of mine, a journalist, is doing an article on an election candidate who may have been mixed up in some scandal over here in the 1970s.'

'Well I was a young man,' said Benady, with a helpful smile. 'Try me.'

'I think it was something to do with the Gibraltar and Atlantic General Trading Company.'

'Yessss,' replied the lawyer, drawing out the s sound and doing a fair impression of Jeremy Paxman. 'We don't have many scandals in Gibraltar, or many unnatural deaths, but a scandal and an unnatural death are most unusual.'

'Really,' said the intrigued auditor. 'Please go on.'

Benady sat back in his chair and rotated ninety degrees clockwise so he could see out of the window and across the bay to Spain. 'Couldn't tell you exactly when it was, late 1975 or early 1976, it was certainly around about then. I know because Franco had just died, and that was part of the problem. You must remember, Tom, that although relations with Spain are strained even now, in the seventies it was completely different. With the border closed we felt like we were in a state of siege, and, as a consequence, things were less civilised than they are today. Some entrepreneurs thought the death of Franco would bring opportunities and would mean the border would be opened. Many of them speculated, buying warehouses and property near the border crossing, investing in stock, generally preparing for the gates to open. Of course 1975 turned into 1976 and there'd been no change, 1976 became 1977, and so on, until 1985, when the border did open, but by then a lot of people had gone bust and Peter Vassallo was one of them.'

Benady paused to observe a frigate that had entered the bay. Then he rotated back to face Mackay and continued. 'Peter Vassallo was the boss of the Gibraltar and Atlantic General Trading Company, an outfit that had taken the biggest punt of all and had borrowed heavily. He was a popular local businessman, well connected with officials in Franco's regime. He'd a few grocery stores both sides of the border, nothing big, and so looking back it was surprising he'd gambled so heavily on this venture and got the finance to do it. As time went on, and as his stock sat rotting in his warehouses, things must have become desperate, but, amazingly, his bank continued to prop him up and he limped on for months. No one was really surprised when he fell to his death off the top of the Rock – suicide, they said.'

'But that's not what you think, John?'

'Well, off the record, I remember thinking to myself at the time that it was all a bit too neat. Why would he have punted so much on such a risky venture? He must've had a tipoff from someone in Madrid, but then there must have been a change of plan which caught him out.'

'You don't think it was suicide.'

Benady spoke softly. 'Spanish secret service would be my guess – pushed him off the top of the Rock to shut him up. Maybe he was planning to take a few others with him when his company crashed.' Benady checked himself, suddenly conscious he'd left that comfortable, traditional world inhabited only by lawyers and wandered into the realms of fantasy and espionage. 'Of course, this is all pure speculation on my part, Tom, probably all nonsense.'

'I'm sure you're right,' said Mackay. 'You wouldn't happen to remember who the Company's bankers were?'

'I don't, it *was* a long time ago. Listen, I'm no corporate lawyer, but if you're that interested, try the library – they keep all sorts of stuff down there. Statutory records, accounts, company filings, that sort of thing.'

'I might just do that. Thanks again for your time,' said Mackay, as if it had been free.

'I'll call you later in the week to finalise what we discussed earlier,' said Benady.

They shook hands at the large blue double doors, the solicitor smiling broadly at his client as he turned to leave the building. Mackay headed towards Main Street. He could see why his uncle had chosen Benady as his lawyer. Mackay could imagine the pair of rogues sitting on the veranda at Jimenez, drinking cerveza, smoking large – excise-free – Cuban cigars, and devising all manner of barely legal schemes. Mackay had liked him too.

He found Sally loitering around Marks and Spencer. He was relieved that she hadn't bought any duty free and he told her about Benady's 'locals only' warehouse. Mackay then related what Benady had said about the Gibraltar and Atlantic General Trading Company – she suggested they go to the library at once to find out more.

The library, or Garrison Library as it was known, was a fine-looking nineteenth-century building and former officers' club in Governor's Parade. The would-be detectives soon discovered that the building also doubled up as the offices of the Gibraltar Chronicle, which was handy given that they were to spend the early afternoon going through the newspaper's archives.

'I guess your journalist friend had dud information,' said Sally, looking at her watch – their flight was at two and she was keen for them to be on their way. 'C'mon Sherlock, we'd better get back to the hotel and pick up the bags. London's calling.'

'This is all I've found, Sal,' said Mackay, holding out a dog-eared document and a browning newspaper cutting. 'It just really confirms what we suspected already.'

'What is it?' she asked.

'It's the Gibraltar and Atlantic General Trading Company's last set of filed accounts. According to these the company was in great shape and had substantial net assets. We now know that these stock figures in the balance sheet are Mickey Mouse – guess who the auditors were?'

'Are you about to say Blake and Lander?' said Sally.

'Well done, Watson.' Mackay paused to think. 'We might find out who the partner was when we get back to the office – I bet it's Craven.' He paused again. 'Now guess who the company's bankers were, Sal?'

'Would I be mistaken if I said the Southern and London Bank?' she said flippantly.

'No, you wouldn't. The banker has to be Jonathan Bridger. He even told me he'd been posted to Gib in the seventies.'

'So there could be a link,' she said, sounding uneasy. 'What does the newspaper cutting say?'

'It's a report of the inquest into Peter Vassallo's death. A suicide verdict was recorded, but the hack who penned this sounds unconvinced.' Mackay handed her the cutting and she read it.

Gibraltar Chronicle
7 May 1977

Local businessman plunges 300 metres to death to avoid fraud probe

The inquest into the death of local businessman Peter Vassallo recorded a verdict of suicide yesterday. The coroner, Mr Joe Karm, heard evidence that Mr Vassallo, whose company had been experiencing severe financial difficulties, was having a meal in the Mons Calpe restaurant with business associates on the evening of 8 April when he became depressed. The restaurant manager, Mr Lorenzo Cachia, testified that Mr Vassallo had been drinking heavily and had been 'difficult' on several occasions during the evening.

The coroner heard that Mr Cachia saw Mr Vassallo get up from his table after an altercation with one of his associates, and say that he needed some air. Mr Karm was satisfied that Mr Vassallo had then taken his own life.

In his summing up, the coroner said that his conclusion was heavily influenced by the police investigation into Mr Vassallo's business affairs, which commenced shortly after his death. The police concluded that Mr Vassallo's company had been trading fraudulently for some time, and it was possible that Mr Vassallo had personally defrauded the company, the company's creditors and its shareholders.

After the court adjourned, Mr Karm refused to answer questions as to why the two business associates of Mr Vassallo hadn't given evidence in court, and why the police report into the fraud at the Gibraltar and Atlantic General Trading Company hadn't been published.

'Interesting,' said Sally. She pointed across the room. 'There's the photocopier. You copy, I'll cab hail. We'll pick up the bags and drop in at your solicitor's bonded warehouse on the way out to the airport – there's no way I'm missing out on litre bottle of Gordon's for two quid.'

CHAPTER ELEVEN

Monday 28 April 1997 – same day

Mackay got back to the flat in London by 6.30pm and noticed how tidy it was. This concerned him, because he knew Ed couldn't achieve such a high level of cleanliness – it could only mean Atif had been in Putney all weekend instead of visiting his girlfriend in Leeds. As Atif went north every weekend without fail, Mackay was worried that something was amiss.

'Good weekend, you Arab,' said Mackay, with false confidence, cautiously entering the lounge. Mackay had long ago acknowledged Atif as the 'world's worst Muslim'. Indeed, since Imran Khan had retired as a global playboy, Atif had been happy and honoured to wear the crown, but it was unusual even for the 'world's worst Muslim' to be drinking a large Scotch on a Monday night.

'She's dumped me, Tomboy,' came the reply, 'for a van driver from Pontefract. One of the little people.' Mackay couldn't help laughing. Atif was pure Pakistani aristocracy – he'd arrived in London as an undergraduate in the late eighties and had never gone home. Mackay had not met a bigger snob. For Atif to be dislodged by 'one of the little people', as he termed those in socio-economic group D, was hilarious.

'Come off it,' said Mackay. 'It's not as if you and Tracy were exactly matched. You were only shagging her because you can't get anything else.'

'Trace and I had a lot in common,' said Atif, with an attempt at seriousness. 'We shared culture, the arts, philosophy. We were kindred spirits. I'll never get over the loss.' Atif smiled and poured a large whisky into the empty tumbler, which Mackay knew had been placed by the bottle in anticipation of his arrival.

Mackay picked up the drink and sipped. 'Perhaps you'll leave our women alone now.'

Atif laughed. 'Oh yeah, I forgot how successful you were with *your* women, Tomboy – how are you getting on with the lovely Annabel by the way?'

'She's yesterday's news, Mustapha.'

As Atif's hairline had begun to recede quite dramatically, Mackay had taken to calling him Mustapha, or, to give him his full Sunday name, Mustapha Wig.

'Now, let me tell you about *my* weekend,' continued Mackay.

They sat down and Mackay told tell Atif about his dirty weekend in Gibraltar, highlighting the comfortable attractions of Miss Sally Purcell, sparing none of the detail, and embellishing wherever possible.

When Mackay had finished, Atif forced out a loud and lengthy artificial yawn. 'I'm right, though, Tom, you can't get near your *own* women. You've needed to cast your net across the pond – American girls are easy.'

'You wait 'til you clock eyes on Sally, then you'll change your tune.'

Atif yawned again. 'So you're not interested in Annabel anymore then?'

'Not in the slightest,' replied Mackay haughtily.

'I'll just delete the message on the answerphone then,' said Atif, feigning getting up out of his chair.

'What? That won't be necessary,' said Mackay. He picked up his drink and headed for the hall, waiting for Atif's laughter to subside in the lounge before pressing the play button.

'Tom, it's Annabel Mylner.' She sounded excited and it was clear she was in a hurry. 'And it's…Monday at just gone six…sorry to hear about your uncle. Roper told me about it. We missed you this weekend. It's not good news I'm afraid. Our local poll result came out on Friday and I think this seat may have become a marginal. We're all in a state of shock – we're only two points ahead of Labour and three points ahead of the LibDems. Silas has been wonderful, very calm – he said there's no way that Barnes and West Putney will ever fall. The Borough Gazette's even come out against us – it must be that horrible little man from the debate the other night. They're hinting that Silas isn't suitable to be an MP. Silas says that after Thursday he's going to sue them, but at the moment he doesn't want to rock the boat. I know you've probably been travelling all day but can you come round? We're all in a flap here, we've got an important visitor coming, quite unexpected. Listen I've got to go – hope to see you later. Bye.' The message ended. Mackay finished his drink.

'I'm off, Atif,' he shouted through to the lounge. 'Duty calls.'

'Tomboy!' came the reply.

'What?' said Mackay, putting his hand on the front door handle.

'I've decided to vote Labour.'

'But you're a bloody toff.' Mackay paused for a moment, thinking aloud. 'Anyway, who said you're allowed to vote?' Mackay sensed he was being wound up so he hurled a sharp 'Piss off, Mustapha' in Atif's general direction, opened the door, ignored the 'Fuck off, you Imperialist', which came back from the lounge, and set off in the direction of Balfour Street.

Mackay could feel the effects of the whisky as he rounded the corner and approached the nerve centre of the Barnes and West Putney Conservative Party. He was surprised to see a noisy crowd gathered outside the building and what appeared to be TV cameras and journalists milling around. He noticed that, since his last visit, the occupants of the second-floor flat above the tanning shop had stuck a large 'Vote Labour' poster in their front window. He was sorry to have missed the look on Roper's face when that went up. He entered the building and met the agent in the hallway.

'Thanks very much for coming, Tom,' said Roper quickly, grabbing his arm. 'Hope everything went OK in Gibraltar. Would you mind being part of a supportive crowd and cheering when our visitor comes out of the building with Silas? There's plenty of rosettes, placards and things in my room – Annabel will sort you out.'

'Will do, Lawrence,' replied Mackay, 'just got to pop into the little boys' room first.'

Mackay went into the toilet and saw the prime minister standing at the left urinal. Mackay sidled up beside him and began pissing next to him. The noise of the crowd outside and the clamour of the party workers within the building had failed to reach the interior of the Balfour Street Gentlemen's toilets, so, other than the sound of gently trickling liquid, it was strangely quiet and peaceful.

After a few moments, Major finished urinating but continued to stand facing the wall. Mackay sensed a prime ministerial unwillingness to go back out into the happy throng, the Balfour Street gentlemen's toilets providing the Brixton boy with a brief respite from the multitude. Mackay finished his own business and walked over to the washbasins, where Major soon joined him. Mackay turned to him and saw the man behind the public face – seven difficult years in office had left their mark, and he looked absolutely knackered.

The pair of Tories continued to wash their hands in awkward silence. Mackay looked at the prime minister again, and he looked back at him. As if they were somehow joined at the hip, they moved in unison to the only paper towel dispenser. Mackay got there first, but he attempted to pull too many towels through the gap and they got stuck. Eventually, he wrestled some free.

Mackay had been staring and he suddenly became aware that the prime minister was staring back at him, somewhat embarrassed. Mackay said the first thing that popped into his head. 'Election going well then, is it?'

The prime minister's eyes twinkled, the corners of his mouth quivered, and he began to giggle, then he giggled some more, then the giggle became a chuckle, which soon became a laugh, and within a few seconds the pair of Tories were roaring with laughter.

'Very…very…very…'said Major, unable to continue through the laughter, 'very well, thanks.'

As the bizarre hilarity of the moment began to subside, Mackay studied him more closely and saw that the burdens of office were gradually slipping from him - here was a man more than anyone else looking forward to Friday morning.

'Well, if things don't go to plan,' said Mackay mischievously, 'why not ignore the result. Give the generals a call today and make sure they're on side - I'm happy to set up a few barricades across Westminster Bridge on Friday morning if you want.'

'OK,' said Major. 'I'll ask Norma to remind me to bring my pitchfork down from Huntingdon.'

'Are you ready, Prime Minister,' came a loud voice from the other side of the door.

'Seriously, though,' said Mackay, as Major moved towards the exit, 'good luck on Thursday.'

'Luck's got nothing to do with it, my friend,' said the prime minister, turning back to face Mackay with a genuine smile. 'We're fucked.'

CHAPTER TWELVE

Tuesday 29 April 1997

72 HOURS TO SAVE UNION, SAYS MAJOR
NEW TAIL IN THE LIFE OF HALE-BOPP
NEW GOALKEEPER IS A GIVEN FOR NEWCASTLE

Mackay arrived early at Connaught Lane. He went up to the third floor and got the files from the locked cupboard. He looked around and saw that everything was as he'd left it the previous Friday.

He settled down at the boardroom table and grabbed the phone. He called Craven's secretary Sarah but as usual she didn't know where Craven was or when he'd be in. Then Mackay called the offices of the Borough Gazette and was told there was no sign of Nick Steadman, and that nobody knew where he was. Added to this, he'd seen that Bridger wasn't about

He got up and walked out of the room towards Bridger's secretary. 'Morning, June. Hope you had a good weekend?'

She spun round in her chair to face him. 'Great thanks – bit bored of this election though, seems to dominate everything.'

Mackay nodded. 'Yes, it's everywhere. We're nearly there though.' He paused. 'Any sign of Jonathan?'

'Sorry, I don't know where he is.'

'It's pretty difficult doing an audit without a managing director or a partner, June,' said Mackay with a smile.

'Yes, he's not been in much lately,' agreed Paterson. 'Must be something to do with the merger.'

'Have those policemen made much progress in finding the hit-and-run driver?' he asked.

'Not that I've heard…' She broke off as the boardroom phone rang. Mackay went to get it.

He picked up the receiver. 'Good morning, Blake and Lander, Tom Mackay speaking.' He expected to hear Craven's clipped voice but, instead, the noise coming from the other end was deafening – he moved the phone away from his ear.

'You anglicised bastard, Mackay, you gone completely native now?' said the voice, in a soft but loud Edinburgh accent, an accent which Mackay thought sounded more English than the speaker would care to admit. 'I knew you'd sell out to the English in the end.'

'What do you want, Rab?' said Mackay apprehensively.

'What, no' how are you, Rab, what've you been up to, Rab, when are you coming down to see me, Rab?'

'What do you want, Rab?' repeated Mackay.

'Well, now you ask, I'm in London on Wednesday – can you put me up? I've got some dreary compliance conference at the Barbican during the day and I fancy a night out in the Smoke. What you doing?'

'Well, in case you hadn't noticed, there's a general election on Thursday and I've been charged with saving the nation from the Reds. I can meet you for a drink in town but that's about it. Of course you're welcome to stay but don't trash the place this time. You still got your key?'

'On a gold chain around my neck, Tommy Boy.'

'What's the political mood like in Edinburgh by the way?'

'Hilarious,' replied Rab. 'Forsyth rarely ventures out of his St Andrew's House bunker, and when he does go out to proclaim doom and gloom about the Tartan Tax, he has to scurry back again sharpish to avoid a lynch mob. The Tories will be wiped out up here I reckon.'

Mackay changed the subject. 'How's the fund management game?' he asked. 'Still fleecing honest folks trying to save for their retirement, and still charging them huge fees to lose their money?'

'God you're a cynic, Thomas,' replied the compliance officer. 'How can we be responsible for unpredictable market movements or senior management failings. Besides, the fees we levy are very reasonable, and naturally enable my colleagues and myself to continue to enjoy the sort of lifestyle to which we've become accustomed. OK, if you'd invested a thousand quid with us two years ago it might be only worth 600 now, but remember you need to benchmark this return against the North Korean Bearer Bond Index. Compared to that, our performance was stellar.'

'Bloody hell,' said Mackay, 'you almost sound as if you believe your own PR. Christ, your snouts are deeper in the City trough than the investment bankers. Your job *is* to spot unpredictable market movements and bad management, that's why you're paid so handsomely.'

Anderson bellowed out a laugh. 'Come come now, Tom, you can't really expect us to return our fees if we lose other people's money, you'll be asking us to get rid of our dart boards next.'

'Good day to you, Mr Anderson,' continued Mackay. 'I hope you choke on your in-flight lobster and Krug on the way down.'

Mackay hung up. Despite getting a third-class degree, Anderson had somehow blundered his way into the compliance industry just as it was becoming fashionable. BCCI and Barings had increased demand for trained buffoons like him, and this need was likely to continue as long as executives felt tempted to put their fingers in the till or break the rules. Anderson was happy to jump on the gravy train just like everybody else, but his defence of the fund management industry wasn't serious.

On the occasions when Mackay had met fund managers, both through Anderson and via his audit work, he'd been astonished to discover that, despite regularly losing other people's money, they all believed that they added value. Mackay farted loudly. The thought of Anderson and his colleagues had been enough to move his bowels, so, without delay, he headed for the third-floor gents.

When he returned, he saw that Bridger was at his desk with his back to the door, talking on the phone. By the time Mackay had sat down, the banker had started another call, which Mackay immediately realised was to one of those new telephone banks.

'Jonathan Bridger,' came the voice from next door. '7 May 1945,' continued the banker, 'Little Mill, East Chirnside, Kelso, Roxburghshire. Yes, the account number is 763821.'

Now for the password, thought Mackay. He knew Bridger had two children, Steven and Yvette, and that his wife's name was Victoria. Would a security conscious banker choose a family name as a password?'

'V,' said Bridger. Had Mackay guessed right? 'E,' continued the banker. So that cuts out his wife, thought Mackay. 'T.' There was a long pause as the other caller confirmed the accuracy of the verification. This was accepted and Bridger gave instructions to move £100,000 to another account. Mackay's immediate thought was that this sum formed part of the insurance rebate and that Bridger, sensing that the net was closing in, was moving it offshore.

The phone rang in the boardroom and Mackay picked it up. 'Blake and Lander,' he said. As he spoke, Bridger spun round in his chair and looked directly at him through the glass partition. He looked back at Bridger and held his stare. 'Did you hear my phone call?' was in Bridger's eyes. 'I might have,' was in Mackay's.

'Tom, are you still there?' It was the departmental secretary, Erica Quirke.

'Yes,' he replied curtly, his gaze still fixed on Bridger.

'That fax you were after has arrived,' said Quirke. 'What do you want me to do with it?'

Mackay picked up Caspian's internal phone book and broke off his Bridger stare. He found the fax number of the credit department and gave Erica the number – it was too risky to use the fax outside the boardroom which he shared with Bridger. He sensed Bridger swing round in his chair and face his desk. What will he do now thought Mackay? Does he know what I'm up to?

Through the half-open door, Mackay heard a fax phone ringing across the floor in the credit department. He left the boardroom and casually walked towards the fax. He saw out of the corner of his eye that

Bridger now had his back to him. The MD was sitting motionless, facing the brick wall in front of him. Don't turn around please, thought Mackay, as he saw the familiar Blake and Lander fax header begin to appear from the depths of the fax machine.

Avon and General
Insurance
23–27 Bernard Street
BRISTOL
BS8 6NE
Tel. 0117 909 6000
Fax. 0117 909 6001

Mr Jonathan Bridger
Managing Director
Caspian Credit Ltd
No. 2 Connaught Lane
Westminster
LONDON
London SW1 4RQ

15 March 1992

Dear Jonathan

Caspian Credit Ltd
Master Credit Insurance – Policy No. Cf/89/76
Profit Share Payment

Further to our telephone conversation of yesterday, I am pleased to confirm that the profit share payable to Caspian Credit Ltd under the terms of Policy CF/89/76 is £7,016,232.67. Further to your instructions, I also confirm that the above sum has been remitted to the Gibraltar and West Mediterranean Bank, account no. 763821……

Mackay read no further. Bloody hell, he thought, this is serious – where was the £7 million now? Was it still in account no. 763821? Was Bridger acting alone? Surely the account would need two signatures. Was Platt's death just a coincidence?

Mackay was anxious. He quickly photocopied the document and wrote in the corner of the photocopy, 'to be given to Detective Inspector Woodhouse (c/o New Scotland Yard) if anything unusual should happen to me.' He dated it and put it in an envelope addressed to himself care of his parents' house. On his way to Bridger's office, he popped the envelope into Caspian's outgoing mail.

Without saying a word, Mackay sat down opposite Bridger and handed him the fax. The banker flexed the fax between his thumb and forefinger several times before starting to read it. When he'd finished, he handed it back to Mackay and looked directly at him.

'It's a mistake,' said Bridger aggressively. 'I know of no such rebate.'

'Has Caspian ever had an insurance policy with Avon and General?' said Mackay evenly.

'Not to my knowledge,' replied Bridger.

'I have further correspondence addressed to you from Avon and General in the early 1990s,' continued Mackay. 'Why is that, do you think?'

'Perhaps the roof sprang a leak and we made a claim,' said Bridger flippantly.

Mackay felt out of his depth. Perhaps this had been a cock-up by Avon and General after all, and he was simply wasting his client's time and fracturing his relationship with Bridger.

Mackay looked closely at Bridger, who stared back at him. 'OK, I'm sorry to have wasted your time with this, but I feel I should pass it on to Inspector Woodhouse as it could be vital to his investigation.'

Mackay saw Bridger shift uneasily in his chair – so perhaps not an error by Avon and General after all, he thought.

Bridger decided to go on the offensive. 'Don't you think you should consult your boss before informing the police? If that fax is genuine, and I'm not saying it is, it means you and your colleagues have missed a large fraud. This is, after all, only a small company. Where can £7 million simply have vanished to?'

Mackay didn't feel intimidated. 'You tell me, Jonathan. You're the MD.'

Bridger took time to think, then continued in a flat, slow tone. 'Let's just for the sake of argument say that the whole £7 million, plus interest, had, as of today, all been completely repaid. Let's say that the money had simply been misplaced, and had never gone missing. What may have happened for example is that a foolish individual, an ageing banker perhaps, had piled into property in the late eighties and got stung. Perhaps that banker needed several hundred thousand pounds to keep him liquid, only until the property market had recovered of course, which it now has.'

'Why would this ageing banker need £7 million then?' probed Mackay.

'Far easier to hide no rebate than part of a rebate,' replied Bridger.

'Hidden until this year that is.' Mackay paused. 'How did Platt pick this up?'

Bridger looked uncomfortable. 'No idea. He should have been a copper that one.'

Mackay pressed on. 'Did he challenge you on it?'

'Yep, I just passed it on to Silas. He discussed it with him.'

There was a pause as both Scotsmen took stock of the situation.

So Craven knew, thought Mackay. It was Mackay who continued first. 'And the hit-and-run, Platt's death I mean, purely a coincidence right?'

Bridger's jaw dropped at this – he looked shaken. 'You don't surely think I'd anything to do with that do you? Who do you think I am?' His denial was robust enough to seem genuine and Mackay believed him. There was a silence as each man pondered what would happen next.

'What will you do now?' said Bridger, speaking his mind. 'Whistleblowers don't come out of these situations well, you know. If you go to the police, your own firm and my bank will sue you for breach of confidentiality. On the other hand, I'm sure the three of us can come to some sort of arrangement.' He paused and let the words hang in the air. 'After all, nothing's actually been stolen, has it?'

Mackay paused and looked closely at Bridger. 'You're lucky the property markets bounced back, otherwise a cover-up wouldn't be an option.'

'Quite,' said Bridger. There was another pause. Mackay fiddled with the Avon and General fax and Bridger flicked his biro on and off repeatedly.

Mackay broke the silence. 'So Silas knows about this. Has he benefited?'

'Not to my knowledge,' replied Bridger. 'He's just helping out an old chum.'

Mackay wasn't convinced. 'That's not like him. Is this anything to do with Gibraltar?' Mackay saw he'd really connected with this one. Bridger's head recoiled three inches as soon as the words had left Mackay's lips.

'Er...Gibraltar,' floundered Bridger, 'how do you know about that?'

'A journalist friend has been digging around and come up with some scandal he was involved with in the seventies. Know anything about that?'

'Er, no,' said the banker feebly. 'If you've got any questions on Gibraltar you'd better ask Silas himself – I know very little about what went on then.' Bridger stopped flicking his pen and put it in his jacket pocket. He saw Inspector Woodhouse come out of the door by the lift. 'Listen, you'd better decide what you want to do quickly,' he said urgently. 'I've an appointment with Inspector Plod.'

Mackay turned in his chair and saw the policeman heading towards them. 'Give me your home number, I'll call you tonight.' Bridger brought a business card out of his desk drawer and scribbled a number on the back of it. Mackay picked it up and put it in his wallet as the policeman knocked at the door.

'Come in, Inspector,' said Bridger, 'we're just finishing.'

Mackay got up to leave. Inspector Woodhouse looked at him. 'Anything unusual cropped up yet, Tom?' asked the policeman.

'No, just the normal number crunching,' replied Mackay credibly.

Mackay looked at Bridger, then left.

CHAPTER THIRTEEN

Tuesday 29 April 1997 – the same day

The phone rang before Steadman had a chance to finish his Benjy's coffee. He picked it up.

'Mr Steadman?'

'Yes.'

'It's Anne Gill here – we met last Friday.'

Steadman imagined her in the sunroom of her Northumberland cottage, cup of tea in hand. 'How are you, Anne? Did you have a good weekend?'

'Yes, thank you. Look, I'll come straight to the point – I think you should come back here. Your visit got me thinking and I've been rummaging about the hall all weekend trying to find Penny's journal. I've found it, and I think you should read it.'

'That's great, Anne, but can't you post it down?' said Steadman, already thinking about his bloated expenses claim. 'I promise I'll look after it.'

'No. I'm not comfortable doing that, Nick. It's not mine, and I doubt if I'm supposed to have it. Besides, there's somebody else who'd like to talk to you about Silas Craven – Old Joe thinks he's remembered something.'

'OK, Anne, sounds intriguing. I'll just clear it with my boss and head up. If I can get away soon, I should be with you late afternoon.'

'Come straight to the cottage when you get here. I'll bake some more scones for you. Bye.'

'Bye, Anne.'

Steadman put down the phone and headed into Metcalfe's office. The office was empty so he turned towards the door, but a rustling of paper from behind the desk halted him.

'Hello,' he said apprehensively.

'Is that you, Nick?' came the editor's reply. 'I'm over here. My back's gone again.'

'Golf or squash this time?' said Steadman, peering over the desk at the horizontal Metcalfe.

'Golf. The sweetest four iron I've ever hit - worth every second of pain.'

'You must be in a good mood then. Any objection if I head north again? I've had a call from that old woman I told you about on the phone - says she's found a journal that will dig the dirt on Craven.'

Metcalfe half-turned to look at Steadman and winced with pain. 'When are you thinking of going?'

'Well, I'll have to go now if we want anything for Thursday.'

'I see.' Metcalfe hesitated. 'Anything from that bean counter who went to Gibraltar - Craven's sidekick?'

'You mean Tom Mackay. No, I haven't spoken to him yet.'

Metcalfe paused again. 'OK, you whiz up, but try and get the last train back to avoid a hotel bill.' Metcalfe tried to turn onto his side but instead grimaced and gave up.

'Don't worry, Roger - I'll be back before you know it.'

Steadman returned to his desk and saw there'd been a phone message from Mackay. He called the number written on the post-it but there was no reply. He flicked through his recently acquired GNER timetable and noted there was a train leaving at 11.50.

This time, his run to King's Cross was quick and uneventful, and Steadman was soon on the train, which set off punctually. Unlike the previous Thursday, the train was on time all the way, and he arrived at Alnmouth at 3.30. Steadman was the only passenger to get off and he was greeted by the same grey-whiskered station master with the green flag. It was clear that the station master had a poor memory for faces when he asked, 'Come far sir?'

'London,' replied Steadman.

'Thought so - you look like you need a holiday,' came the stock reply.

'OK, I'll take it easy then.' Steadman nodded towards the departing intercity. 'Does the train always run on time when it's in old BR livery?' he asked mischievously.

'Always,' said the station master. 'I'm still waiting for the private sector benefits to filter through. As long as they don't muck about with my pension I don't care – I've only got three years to go.'

'Maybe Labour will renationalise it on Friday morning,' said Steadman.

'Maybe,' said the station master, distracted by the southbound 15.35 as it rounded the bend.

Steadman left him and walked to Alnmouth. Given the sexual benefits that might be available at the Schooner Hotel that night, Steadman had no intention of catching the last London-bound train, so the first thing he did was check in. He was disappointed to find the reception desk manned by the cheeky young barman-cum-waiter instead of Judith.

'It's Judith's day off,' he said slyly, before Steadman could ask where she was. 'She'll be in later though – she always has her nights off in the bar.'

'Thanks,' said Steadman, caught between picking up the room key and clipping the cheeky lad behind the ear. He took the key and dropped his overnight bag in his room, then headed towards Keeper's Cottage.

Steadman's route took him past the Dower House – as he drew level with the building, he saw Craven's mother sitting in the large bay window, drinking tea. She saw him instantly and gave him a frosty look before picking up the phone and dialling. Although he couldn't hear anything, Steadman was sure she was calling her son.

While Spring had arrived in the capital, Winter was having a last kick in the north east, and the air brought on shore from the North Sea by the strong easterly wind was cold. The temperature contrast between the exterior and interior of Keeper's Cottage couldn't have been more marked, and Steadman was soon wrapped in the comfortable old armchair, tea in one hand, dribbly scone in the other.

'Now, Nick,' said Anne Gill, her green eyes infusing him with her life force, 'there it is.' She handed him a large, leather-bound journal. 'Finish your scone first, though – I don't want you dropping butter on it.'

Steadman stuffed the remainder of the scone into his mouth and began to read. The early years were the stuff of ordinary little rich girls, of horses, grand houses, hunting, shooting, fishing and glittering balls held in draughty castles. The journal described the early death of her mother and her father's appointment of a housekeeper shortly afterwards. The housekeeper's husband, Alan Craven, had been killed in a mining accident the previous year, so the offer of employment, while genuine, also had charitable motives.

Mrs Craven had a son, Silas, who, as the years went by, became one of the family. While Penny's brother David enjoyed the physical side of farming, he had no aptitude for the estate's administration, whereas Silas was gifted with numbers and a good organiser. Indeed, so successful was he at managing the estate that it showed a small profit for the first time in years.

It was only natural that David began to feel threatened and his relationship with Silas began to deteriorate. Things got much worse during the spring of 1963 when Silas and Penny returned from Gretna Green married. David and Silas's differences became irreconcilable, so Basil was forced to offer them an estate cottage and secure Silas a position at a local accountancy firm. It was here, at 31 December 1963, that the journal ended.

Steadman hid his disappointment. 'Very interesting,' he said, 'but to be honest not a great deal of journalistic value in here, Anne.'

'But where's the rest of it?' replied the nonagenarian rhetorically. 'Where's 1964? Where's the last seven months of her life? I've looked all over the hall but I can't find it anywhere. She must've hidden it to keep it away from Craven. Joe thinks he knows where it might be. He'll meet you in the Schooner at eight.'

'OK,' said Steadman, stumbling as the armchair springs propelled him forward forcefully as he stood. 'I'll let you know if I find anything out.'

When he opened the door to leave, the wind blew in with such ferocity that several lace doilies took off, and Mrs Gill's husband made one last flight across the room, almost shattering the glass in the photo frame as he crash landed on the floor.

'Stay away from the cliff path in this wind,' she warned, before closing the door.

The short walk back to the hotel took longer than usual as Steadman was forced to lean into the wind all the way. Even with the heavy oak door to the Schooner firmly closed behind him, the wind still whistled through the bar, lifting the browning pennants and rattling the rusted anchors.

There was no sign of Judith or Old Joe. Steadman tried to avoid conversation with the cheeky young barman while he pulled his pint. 'Maybe Jude's not coming in tonight,' said the youth with feigned concern.

'OK,' said Steadman, trying to sound disinterested, but feeling foolish when a beer mat stubbornly refused to disengage itself from the bottom of his pint glass. Before he'd had a chance to pay, he caught a glimpse of a blue peaked cap of the Uncle Albert style out of the corner of his eye.

'I'll have a Federation please, son,' said the blue peaked cap.

They sat in the same wooden booth they'd sat in the previous week – Joe had drunk half his pint before he spoke again. 'Of course, when we met the other day, I didn't think to tell you I'd seen Penny Gray that night – the night she died. It was a night much the same as this, a gale force wind, but warmer. I was up at the castle watching the boats come in when she scurried by. I didn't really notice at the time, but meeting you last week and talking to old Anne Gill reminded me that she was carrying some sort of book. I never thought to mention it at the time given the police were so certain it was an accident, but now I'm not so sure. What happened to that book? There was no sign of it when they found the body.'

'Perhaps she hid it in the castle, Joe,' said Steadman. He paused. 'Why were the police so sure it was an accident?'

'No motive for anything else. As far as the village was concerned, Penny and Craven had the perfect marriage, and she didn't hide her book in the castle – I would have seen.'

Steadman wasn't convinced. 'What's further along the path?'

Joe thought for a moment. 'Nothing really. Nothing until you get to Craster. Just a few Second World War bunkers.' He paused again. 'She could have hidden it in one of them. I remember she and her brother used to play in the nearest one when they were kids.'

'How far past the castle is it?' said the journalist, rising to his feet.

'Leave it 'til the morning,' said Joe, looking alarmed. 'It'll be dark soon and the path will be treacherous in this wind.'

Steadman smiled. 'Don't worry about me, Joe. I was in the Boy Scouts you know.'

He began to regret his decision even before he'd left the bar. It took three heaves to open the heavy oak door, which seemed locked by the strength of the wind, and, once in the street, the wind tried to blow him into the path of a bus, only missing him by a whisker.

The path up to the castle was more sheltered but the noise was incredible. The intense howling of the wind was interrupted at regular intervals by a deafening thud from the block-hole, which sent huge plumes of seawater crashing over the walls and onto the path.

Steadman was soon wet with spray as he half stumbled and half slipped down the path at the far side of the castle. He saw that the tide was out. This was fortunate as it meant he could cut across the pebbly beach onto the next headland. In the half light, he could see a concrete pill box silhouetted against the skyline in front of him. Joe had told him there'd been a scare in 1940 that Hitler might come from Norway, so hundreds of these pill boxes had been built, more as observation posts than as serious defensive structures.

The rear part of the pillbox had been dug into the side of the bank. It took Steadman several minutes to find a narrow trench, which led to an even narrower door sunk low into the concrete. He crawled in on his hands and knees. It was dark inside and reeked of urine. He flicked on his cigarette lighter and saw instantly that he was in the right place – the initials 'DG' and 'PG' had been carved into the concrete with the date '17 March 1956'. He knew at once that the missing diary was buried under the pile of stones in the corner of the pillbox.

After a couple of minutes of scratching around he found it, wrapped in a greasy canvas bag and tied up with twine. It was difficult holding his cigarette lighter and taking notes as he read, but there was still some light coming from the slit at the front of the pillbox, and he was completely sheltered from the wind.

By the time the flame flickered and died with the last of the lighter fluid, he'd jotted down most of what he needed. He peered out of the machine gun slit and saw there was very little light left. The sea was a mass of white splashes as the wind continually whipped up the surf – no way the Wehrmacht would have been coming tonight, he thought, as he turned to crawl out of the pillbox.

As he stood and looked towards the castle, which, in the semi-darkness, appeared to bar his way home, he saw a torch flicker from within the gatehouse. Another idiot out on a night like this, thought Steadman, as he slid down the path onto the pebbly beach.

By the time he'd crossed the bay and started to climb towards the castle it was so dark that he could barely see the path. The lights from the village pointed to the general direction, but the path seemed intent on traversing every slippery rock and deep ditch in the county. The wind howling through the ramparts was incessant, and the continuous thud from the block-hole sounded like a barrage.

Steadman made his way cautiously through the compound until the path narrowed once again between the wall and the cliff edge. Even in the daylight it was doubtful whether Steadman would have seen the stocky man hunched in the gatehouse. So, when he half-turned to face the man after his notebook and journal had been snatched, he was caught off balance, and the wind blew him over the edge onto Greymare Rocks.

CHAPTER FOURTEEN

Tuesday 29 April 1997 – the same day

As soon as he'd finished parrying Inspector Woodhouse's ineffectual questions, Bridger picked up his briefcase and headed out of the office. 'I'll finish this report at home, June,' he said unconvincingly, as he passed his secretary on the way out of the building.

Once outside, he turned left and walked behind the Army and Navy Stores. He skirted by Westminster Cathedral and arrived at the Edwardian Mansion block that served as his weekday home. The one-bedroom flat was sparsely decorated and reflected its status as a place to stay rather than a home.

Bridger looked at the pictures of his wife and children in the alcove next to the gas fire. He took off his jacket, kicked off his shoes and poured himself a large Highland Park from the already open bottle.

Mackay's questioning had unsettled him. It had never occurred to the banker that Platt's death might not have been an accident – could it be linked to the insurance rebate? If it was murder, then there was only one suspect, but Silas had been with him the Friday night that Platt had died. Was Silas up to hiring a contract killer? The thought was preposterous, but Bridger knew Craven could be ruthless. He thought back to the scandal in Gibraltar and Peter Vassallo's death.

Bridger had arrived in Gibraltar freshly promoted to manager of the bank's branch. The position was the first he'd had with any real responsibility, and, in those days, branch managers did have real responsibility. As well as finding new business, he was tasked with approving new credit lines, so, towards the end of his first year in charge, when he was just short of his annual target, Peter Vassallo had walked in with the rosiest business plan that Bridger had ever seen. It was a licence to print money.

At that time, every item sold in Gibraltar came in by air or sea, so, when Franco died, and the prospect of cheap goods flooding in by land became a reality, Bridger was convinced that the bank should jump onto the bandwagon along with everybody else. His quick appraisal of Vassallo's trading history revealed solid year-on-year growth. The accounts were audited and signed off by Blake and Lander, and Vassallo himself was plausible and trustworthy - a good businessman. As the requested £50,000 was within his own authority limits, Bridger approved the loan and remitted the funds himself.

A month later, Bridger saw Vassallo at a New Year's Eve party given by the governor at the Convent. Vassallo was in the corner of the room, gesticulating wildly at another man, who stood motionless, absorbing the Gibraltan's malevolence. As Bridger approached, they abruptly broke off their conversation and turned to greet him. Vassallo became all sweetness and light. The other man remained expressionless.

'Ah, my good friend Jonathan Bridger,' said Vassallo, 'allow me to introduce you to my accountant, Silas Craven.'

'Nice to meet you,' said Craven, taking the banker's hand. 'I understand Peter is our mutual client.'

'Yes,' said Bridger evenly. He had been disconcerted by Vassallo's intemperate behaviour and felt concerned that the conversation had ended abruptly as he'd approached. Bridger looked more closely at Craven and saw a man with film-star looks, more elegant than Clark Gable yet no Cary Grant - a mix.

There was an uncomfortable silence. Bridger looked at his shoes and was glad when the group of acolytes surrounding the governor roared into laughter, giving him the chance to look at something other than his feet. When the laughter died down, there was a second silence.

It was Craven who spoke first, and, as he spoke, he smiled so warmly at Bridger that the words that left his lips, words which Bridger had been half-expecting, seemed to be coated with sugar.

'There may be a problem with your loan,' said the accountant. He paused, letting the full impact of every banker's nightmare sink in.

'Oh,' said Bridger weakly.

'The thing is,' continued Craven, 'the border isn't going to be opened this year, and Peter's got a lot of rotting stock in his warehouses. I'm afraid most of it will have to be written off.'

In just a few seconds, Bridger's career had fallen apart – he was stunned. 'How much is left of the fifty thousand?' he asked.

'Not much,' replied Vassallo. 'Most of it's been used to pay off the trade creditors – I'll struggle to meet January's wage bill.'

'Christ!' said the wretched banker slowly. 'You've really stitched me up.' Bridger thought of his twelve years of hard slog at the bank and how it lay rotting along with Vassallo's putrefying stock. He lashed out at the two nearest targets. 'I won't go down alone for this!'

Craven took a step towards him and put his hand on his arm, holding it tightly. The accountant looked the banker directly in the eye and gave him one of his syrupy smiles. Bridger looked away, unable to hold his stare.

'There's no need to do anything hasty,' said Craven comfortingly. 'There'll be a solution to this problem.'

The solution was to throw more money at the Gibraltar and Atlantic General Trading Company. As the documentation for the original £50,000 loan was still on Bridger's desk, it was easy to issue a new loan agreement showing a £75,000 loan payable in two tranches. Bridger remitted the second tranche of £25,000 shortly before the end of January, at the same time as Craven certified the company's accounts.

Bridger never had discovered why Craven had been so helpful to Vassallo. Bridger had relied on Blake and Lander's opinion when he'd advanced the original loan, but Craven could have wriggled out of that. He was sure Vassallo had some other hold over him.

Things went smoothly for the next few months. Before Vassallo's gamble on the border crossing had gone wrong, his company had traded reasonably well, so he was able to service the debt and

Bridger even began to think that, given time, some capital repayments might be possible. These hopes were dashed in September of that year when Vassallo and Craven came into his office.

It was a hot day and Bridger could see that Vassallo was sweating profusely through his open-necked shirt. The businessman looked haggard but excitable. He opened his briefcase and slapped an all-too-familiar business plan on Bridger's desk. Without hesitating, the banker pushed the document back to him.

'No way,' said Bridger. 'No more money.'

'But Jonathan,' began Vassallo, 'we are such good friends. We need each other. The border will open this time and I will repay your money – we will all be rich.'

'No,' said Bridger forcefully. 'Even if I wanted to, a fresh loan so soon would raise eyebrows at Head Office.' He looked at Craven for support but none came. Instead, Vassallo continued.

'But I've been so good to you these last few months, Jonathan. We've had a lot of fun, have we not?' Vassallo's meaning was clear. While Bridger hadn't taken a bribe as such, there had of course been perks. He had eaten in the best restaurants this side of Paris, paid for nothing, and enjoyed, on a temporary basis, the company of one beautiful woman after another.

'Are you threatening me, Peter?' asked Bridger calmly.

'Not at all, Jonathan, I'm merely pointing out that the three of us have formed a close bond.' He paused to choose his words carefully. 'It would be difficult to see how we could survive as individuals if those bonds were…er…fractured.'

There was silence, then Vassallo pushed the business plan back to Bridger. Craven, who had sat expressionless up to this point, interjected, 'Let's not be hasty now. Why don't we let Jonathan have a think about our proposal and revisit the subject tomorrow, over dinner at the Mons Calpe.'

The businessman and the banker nodded their heads in agreement and all three men got up to awkwardly shake hands. Bridger looked at Vassallo then at Craven. Craven tipped his head slightly as he took Bridger's hand. 'Don't worry about it, Jonathan, I'll sort this out.'

Bridger got up from his seat and poured himself another large Highland Park. There was a draught coming through the kitchen door, which was ajar, so he closed it and turned up the gas fire to maximum before settling down again in his armchair, his thoughts returning to 1970s Gibraltar.

When Craven had said, 'I'll sort this out,' it *had* crossed Bridger's mind at the time that Vassallo's death had been remarkably convenient. Sure, by the time Vassallo had entered the Mons Calpe restaurant he was very drunk, and it had always seemed more likely to Bridger that he'd stumbled and fallen, rather than jumped off himself. But now he wasn't so sure.

It later transpired that Vassallo and Craven had been drinking all day, but Craven had appeared sober to Bridger. As soon as they'd arrived at the restaurant, the subject of the loan was brought up and the conversation had quickly become heated, but without the professional restraint of the previous day. Vassallo had, in turns, become aggressive, then conciliatory, then morose, but never suicidal.

Craven had looked on impassively as the Gibraltan delivered his drunken diatribe against the Spanish, bankers, and the British. When Vassallo got up for a piss and Craven followed him out for a cigar, it had never occurred to Bridger that Craven had had anything to do with Vassallo's permanent failure to return.

The subsequent investigation had been lightweight, hinting at a desire to suppress any financial scandal to suggest that the dependency couldn't regulate itself. Could Craven have pushed Vassallo off the top of the Rock, calmly walked back to the table, poured himself another brandy, then courteously asked after the health of Bridger's family? It seemed incredible.

Bridger's recollections were abruptly interrupted by the buzzer to the external door. He got up, walked to the internal phone and picked it up.

CHAPTER FIFTEEN

Wednesday 30 April 1997

HESELTINE WARNS NATION SLEEPWALKING TO DISASTER
MAJOR SAYS 'NEW LABOUR' IS A 'GREAT MARKETING SCAM'
MOBUTU TO MEET REBEL LEADER ON SOUTH AFRICAN SHIP

Mackay had slept fitfully and doubted whether he'd had much REM. During the evening he'd tried to call Bridger several times but there'd been no reply. All night, he'd considered what he was going to do. The money had been repaid – the £7 million could still be included in this year's figures – he himself would likely benefit if he kept quiet. Everyone was a winner. Was there really any harm done? The consequences of opening his mouth were dreadful. He would be sacked and sued by both Blake and Lander and Caspian for breaches of confidentiality. Bridger, and perhaps Craven, would go to prison, and the Tory Party would absorb yet another scandal.

He got out of bed and decided that, before doing anything else, he would confront Craven with what he knew. This would serve the dual purpose of hearing Craven's side of things and finding out what was in it for himself if he kept quiet. If there was any fallout and a subsequent witch-hunt, Mackay didn't care what happened to Craven, and the government was doomed anyway. He liked Bridger, but he was more concerned about his own welfare. Who would employ him without references? Nobody liked a whistleblower.

He showered and dressed quickly, then breezed through the kitchen without stopping for breakfast. It was unusual for Mackay to be up before his flatmates, but even more unusual for him to catch the 7.50. He found the earlier hour made a difference and he struggled to get on the train.

Instead of the usual calm hush punctuated by occasional tense conversation, the carriage was completely silent, as each commuter no doubt wondered what impact on them the new government would have. Mackay glanced around the carriage and saw the usual mix of men in grey suits, young City workers and graduate trainees. After eighteen years, were the good times coming to an end? New Labour had few friends on this train, thought Mackay. He saw the platform approach and felt the train slow to a walking pace. The silence and glum faces of Mackay's fellow passengers evoked in his mind images of the French Revolution - was the carriage a tumbril carrying the *ancien regime* to the 'Place de Westminster' where Madame Blair waited patiently with a sharp tax hike?

It was the first time that year that Mackay had beaten Tony King into the office. When the diminutive auditor arrived to see Mackay at his desk, already working, it upset his value system, so much so that, despite opening his mouth to say something, no words came out.

Mackay ignored him and flicked through the internal phone directory. He found Craven's number and dialled. He wasn't surprised when there was no answer. He'll be in the constituency shaking hands and kissing babies, thought Mackay. To make sure, Mackay took the lift up to the sixth floor. Craven's office was empty, but he could see a Burberry overcoat and black umbrella in the room, and Craven's briefcase lay semi-ajar on the mahogany desk - it was clear Craven was putting to the test what the 'safe' in 'safe seat' actually meant.

Mackay took a pen out of his pocket and walked over to the desk, intending to leave Craven a post-it asking him to call when he returned. As Mackay bent down, he glanced into the briefcase and saw a large, green, hard-backed A4 notebook. In the top right-hand corner, emblazoned in silver, were the words 'Borough Gazette'.

Mackay was stunned - what the hell was Craven doing with that? A noise from the corridor prompted him to begin writing. He heard somebody come into the room behind him and turned to face Craven.

'What are you up to, Tom?' said the partner evenly.

'Just leaving you a note,' replied Mackay, a little too quickly.

'About what?'

'Caspian.'

Craven walked past Mackay and sat down at his desk with his back to him. He gently closed his briefcase and pointed to the seat next to him, indicating that Mackay should sit down. Mackay did as he was told and sat at right angles to his boss. Without looking at him, Craven continued with a trace of irritation in his voice. 'What about Caspian?' He paused. 'You know how busy I am at the moment.'

Mackay came straight to the point. 'I've found a £7 million insurance rebate that's been missing for five years.'

Mackay waited for some sort of reaction from Craven, but there wasn't one. Instead, he sat impassively looking out of the window. Mackay's words continued to linger until the phone rang. As the ringing persisted, and as it was clear that Craven wasn't going to answer, Mackay reached forward to pick it up.

'Leave it,' snapped Craven, with such ferocity that Mackay flinched backwards in his chair. They sat in silence and, when the ringing eventually stopped, Craven slowly spun round in his chair to face Mackay full on. There was a black, icy, savage quality to his eyes, which unsettled Mackay and made his earlier boldness evaporate. Craven continued, '£7 million, you say?'

'Yes.'

'Has Jonathan Bridger confirmed this to you?'

'More or less. And besides, I have third-party evidence.' Mackay hesitated before continuing, 'He said that you knew about it. He said Keith Platt had told you.'

'That's a lie,' said Craven softly. It was obvious he'd regained his composure, so Mackay, with a daring unusually alien to him, determined to see if he could rattle Craven again.

'Did you work with Bridger in the seventies?' There was no reply, so Mackay continued, 'have you ever been to Gibraltar, Silas?' Craven gave Mackay his warm treacly smile and drew him in. He was back in control – confident, assured and unflappable.

'What of it, Tom?' he said softly.

'Well, I…he…' blurted out Mackay, 'Bridger, I mean…' Mackay hesitated to gather his thoughts and order the words in his mind. Craven continued to eyeball him – his unremitting stare penetrated Mackay and it felt as though his brain was disconnecting. Had they been on a street corner in Brixton, 'what you looking at?' would have been an appropriate response. Instead, Mackay stumbled on, his attempt to rattle Craven melting away. 'The thing is, Silas, Bridger hinted there may have been some sort of scandal.'

Craven got up from his seat, signifying the meeting was over. As Mackay stood up, Craven put one hand on his shoulder and took his arm with the other. 'The delusions of a has-been banker, Tom. Don't you worry about this insurance rebate or talk of scandal, I'll sort it out. Group have had their suspicions about Bridger for a while now. These sorts of accusations aren't helpful.' He paused and then changed the subject. 'Will I see you at the constituency tonight?'

'Er, maybe, Silas,' replied Mackay, bewildered by the sudden switch to normality. 'I've one or two things to do at home first.'

'Be great if you could make it,' said Craven, further extending his smile to the full yard. 'I do value your support – it will be rewarded.'

With that, Craven closed the door and Mackay was out in the corridor. As the lift descended into the bowels of the building, Mackay pondered on Craven's parting remark. Had there been a hidden meaning there? If there had, did Craven think Mackay came that cheaply? The delusions of a has-been banker, Craven had said, yet Bridger had told Mackay that Craven had known about the £7 million rebate. It seemed more likely that a desperate Bridger had threatened to lift the lid on the Gibraltar scandal, and that, to keep him quiet, Craven had ignored the disappearance of the £7 million.

Mackay arrived back at his own office to find Sally Purcell deep in conversation with Tony King. As he entered the room, they broke off their conversation and she sat down on his desk. King acknowledged Mackay with a grimace and set off in the direction of the coffee machine.

'What were you talking to Wan about?' asked Mackay nonchalantly.

She smiled at him. 'I told him we were an item.'

Mackay was surprised. 'What did he think of that?'

'Fairly shocked. He thinks I should be in mourning and draped from head to foot in black. Besides, I think he was a bit jealous. He fancies me.'

'Christ, is there anybody in this department who doesn't?' Mackay turned to look at her and she smiled at him tenderly. God, she was attractive. He glanced at the semi-open door and was tempted to close it, lock it and jump on her then and there.

'Talking of your admirers, I've got a little job for you.'

'What?'

'I want you to lure Craven out of his office for twenty minutes so I can pinch something out of his briefcase.'

She frowned. 'I hope you're joking. No more conspiracy theories please,' she said firmly.

'Not a theory, my dear, hard evidence. Craven's got that journalist's notebook.' She shifted nervously on the desk, realising that Mackay was serious. Here was a real test of her commitment to him. 'Are you doing any work for him at the moment?' continued Mackay.

'Just a shitty unit trust. I'll need something more to get him to come down here.'

'You'll have to flirt with him then.'

'No, he'd guess something was up. I gave him a big knock-back when he made a pass at me before.' She paused to think. 'He smokes. I'll tell him Keith told me something about the Caspian job and he can meet me outside for a fag.'

Mackay was impressed. 'Brilliant. But you'd better do it quickly – I don't want him scooting off with his briefcase and the journal.' With a seated semi-twirl worthy of Anthea Redfern, she reached out for the phone and picked it up. He saw her dial 0 for the internal switchboard and purse her lips – it was a habit Mackay liked.

'Silas Craven please.' She flicked her hair nervously as she waited to be connected. 'Silas, it's Sally Purcell.' Mackay saw her shift her weight to her left buttock as she listened to the condolences about Platt streaming eloquently from the sixth floor. As the flow subsided, she flicked her hair again and pursed her lips. 'Silas, I really am fine, thank you.' She paused. 'The reason I'm calling is something Keith said to me. It's been troubling me, and I think it might be important.' There was silence. Mackay wished he was a fly on the wall in Craven's office, observing his reaction. Instead, he watched as Sally flicked her hair for the third time and re-pursed her lips. 'I'd rather not talk about it in the building,' she continued. 'Will you meet me at the St Michael's Street exit for a smoke?' There was a short pause and she put the phone down. Craven had agreed. 'What shall I tell him?' she said, performing the reverse seated semi-twirl to bring her back in front of Mackay on the desk.

'Just that Keith mentioned that the seven million quid was bothering him, and that he was going to mention it to Craven. You're just making sure that that information is passed on.'

'What if he tries to push me under a cab?' she said half-seriously.

'Just turn and face it and it'll bounce off,' replied Mackay with a dirty smile.

'For God's sake, be serious, Tom. I don't like this. You and your conspiracy theories. You should have worked for MI5.'

'What conspiracy theories are those then?' said Tony King, walking back into the room, coffee in hand.

'Well thanks for getting us coffees, Tony,' said Sally sarcastically, giving him a sweet smile.

'Er, well, sorry Sal…what do you want?' King put his coffee on the desk and started back towards the door.

'Only joking Mr King,' she said, brushing past him on her way out, 'I'm off on an errand.'

'Me too,' echoed Mackay, and Tony King was left standing motionless, inhaling her scent.

Mackay headed for the sandwich bar on the fourth floor, which was the only part of the building that overlooked the St Michael's Street 'smokers' area.' Mackay saw that the sandwich bar looked the same as it did when he'd last visited, despite having been 'enhanced' since the staff restaurant had closed. It was too early for lunch traffic but the usual collection of journeymen milled around buying 'real' cappuccinos, which were no better than the muck dispensed from the machines.

Mackay propped himself against the floor-to-ceiling window at the far end of the room and looked out over St Michael's Street. There was no sign of Sally amongst the shirt-sleeved smokers who fidgeted uncomfortably between gasps. He saw her come out of the building and stand off one of the smaller groups of men partially secreted in the doorway of a fire exit. None of the men acknowledged her, but Mackay saw one of them subconsciously run his hand through his hair and another move his feet to stand fully astride a manhole cover - they were aware of her presence.

Mackay could see that the taller of the three men, who was closest to her, was toying with the idea of offering her a light. Mackay saw him fumble in his jacket pocket. How many relationships have started like this? he thought. The man's hand reappeared without the lighter, though, as Craven emerged from nowhere and stood aggressively between Sally and the men. Mackay caught a glimpse of Sally flicking her hair and giving Craven her helpless look.

Mackay turned from the window and headed for the stairs. He raced up them two at a time and was soon in the corridor leading to Craven's office. As he approached, he saw Craven's secretary Sarah at the far end of the corridor walking towards him. She would reach the office first. God, I hope she's not going in, thought Mackay, as Sarah caught his eye about twenty feet in front of him and smiled as she turned left into Craven's office. Mackay glanced through the door as he drew level then continued towards the stairs at the other end of the building. A notice board gave him the opportunity of legitimately loitering, as he wondered how long it would take Sarah to finish the note he'd seen her writing on Craven's desk.

Mackay had noted Sarah's plain appearance when he'd first met her the previous week. She had been pleasant, even likeable, but now, every passing minute he stood at the notice board accentuated her unattractiveness. What the hell was she doing in there? Mackay fidgeted as he read the firm's insurance policy, which was pinned to the board, for the sixth time.

Eventually, out of the corner of his eye, he saw her leave the office and shuffle to her own room. He felt guilty about her as he turned and walked calmly back along the corridor and into Craven's office. The briefcase was where it had been earlier but now it was closed – was it locked? Despite his shaking hands, it clicked open and he found the green notebook with the letters NJS written under the Borough Gazette. He pulled it out and closed the lid.

Mackay rapidly retraced his steps to the fourth-floor sandwich bar. He resumed his earlier position and again looked out of the floor-to-ceiling window. Sally was talking to the tall man who'd reached for his lighter but Craven was gone. Mackay shifted a few feet to his right so that he could be seen from the street below. Sally saw him instantly. He gave her the thumbs up and she feigned wiping sweat from her brow. He saw her say something to the tall man, drop her cigarette on the pavement, stub it out with her shoe, then turn and go back into the building. He met her in his empty office a few minutes later and he saw that her face was flushed with excitement. It suited her. 'Well done. What did Craven say?'

'I could see he was interested,' she said, pausing for breath, 'though he did say that Keith had mentioned something about it, which weakens your conspiracy theory a bit.'

Mackay shook his head. 'That's not what he told me. He's probably trying to distance himself from Bridger.' Mackay fingered the journal, wondering what to do next. 'Look, why don't we knock off at five and head back to mine to read this book properly? I'll try the Borough Gazette again to see if they've heard from their boy. Let's keep our heads down until then.'

'Fine,' she replied, heading out of the room, 'let's audit.'

At three o'clock, Mackay tried to get hold of Steadman. He was put straight through to the editor of the Gazette. Mackay detected concern in Metcalfe's voice when he told him he didn't know where Steadman was.

'Have you been helping him with his election coverage?' asked the editor.

'Something like that,' replied Mackay, glancing at the spine of Steadman's notebook, which was visible in his briefcase.

'If he tries to contact you, do me a favour and let me know.' Metcalfe paused. 'It's not like him to go AWOL.'

'Of course,' replied Mackay. Had Craven given Steadman an interview after all and had the journalist simply left his notebook by accident? It seemed unlikely. Mackay thought it more plausible that Craven had something to do with Steadman's disappearance, but that seemed incredible.

At five o'clock, Mackay picked Sally up from her office and together they walked to Waterloo to catch a train to Wandsworth. They missed the 5.20 so decided to use Route B to Clapham Junction and stretch their legs from there.

The walk from the station took longer than usual because they'd to skirt round a mob of Labour supporters who'd surrounded a small group of Tory activists. The outnumbered Tories had flung a thin piquet line around their MP, but the line had been breached in several places, allowing the left-wingers to pelt the besieged parliamentarian with rotten eggs.

'Aren't you going to help them, Tom?' asked Sally, as they avoided a fearsome-looking leather-jacket-clad socialist, who lurched towards them in a Yosser Hughes-like manner.

'Not in my constituency,' replied Mackay. 'We must be in Battersea here. Plus, I'm beyond caring.'

They reached the flat without further incident. Mackay knew that Ed was on a course and there was no sign of Atif – the flat was empty. As Mackay's suggestion that they examine the notebook in bed was flatly refused, they sat down at the kitchen table and leafed through Steadman's unwieldy scribble.

'I know a bit of shorthand, but I'm struggling to decipher this, Tom,' said Sally, after about an hour. 'There's nothing in the longhand to suggest anything odd either. I'm beginning to half believe Craven's side of it. What really surprises me is that he's a Geordie – he's hidden his humble class very well.'

Mackay laughed. 'Only an American would say the word class. You think we still doff caps and bend knees like your lot did before you got rid of King George.'

'You still refer to working class,' she said. 'I hear it in the press all the time.'

He paused to think. 'It's a good point. But we're all working class now – we all work. There aren't many toffs left who do nothing all day but beat their serfs.'

She hesitated. 'When I go back to the States, why don't you come with me and see what a real meritocracy is like?'

She said it without raising her head from the journal. Mackay was surprised. He looked at her but she didn't move – avoiding his eyes.

Before he could answer, she sat bolt upright. 'Look,' she said excitedly, pointing to some clear lettering amidst the jumble of squiggles and dashes. 'Craven was shagging his secretary.'

'The dirty bastard.'

'Shagging and impregnating by the look of it,' said Sally, reading further on.

'The dirty bastard,' repeated Mackay. He paused then voiced his jumbled thoughts. 'Craven's wife's family were devout Catholics and pillars of the local community. This would have been a scandal. Things have changed a lot since the sixties but this still won't go down well with the Barnes and West Putney Blue Rinse Brigade. No wonder Penny Gray was pissed off when she found out he was getting his leg over at work. Maybe he pushed her off the cliff to keep her quiet. This certainly gives him a motive, but it doesn't prove he killed her.'

'No,' agreed Sally. 'I wonder what happened to the baby.'

'I don't know, but we'll likely be seeing pictures of it in the Borough Gazette soon. What shall we do now, Sal?'

'Nothing. We do nothing. We wait for Steadman to turn up then compare notes with him. This doesn't seem to be related to Gibraltar in any way.'

'No it doesn't,' he said, stifling a yawn. 'Listen, these hieroglyphics are giving me a headache. Why don't we drop it for now and go grab something to eat.'

'No can do, lover,' she replied. 'I'm off out with the girls tonight.'

'Oh,' mouthed a surprised Mackay. 'Where are you off to?'

'The movies.'

'To see what?'

'The Full Monty, of course. Can't miss a full frontal of Robert Carlyle now, can I?'

Mackay caught up with her as she opened the door. She seemed embarrassed about inviting him to America and keen to get away – he decided not to mention it. He kissed her.

'Well, I'll see you tomorrow in the office then,' he said glumly. 'And Sal?'

'What?'

'Don't forget to vote.'

The joke was weak and she turned to face him. 'Rest assured, Thomas…' She paused, lingering over her next words. 'If I was allowed to vote in this backwater of a country, I'd be cancelling your vote out.' Then she left.

Mackay stood still, staring at the closed door.

Five minutes later, there was a knock at the door. Mackay walked towards it, glad that Sally had changed her mind - a full frontal of himself proving more appealing than Robert Carlyle.

He flung the door open and instinctively flinched backwards as one of the men threw a punch at his stomach, but Mackay hadn't recoiled enough and the blow connected. He yelled and doubled over, completely winded. He heard the door close just as the second strike landed on his neck, spreading intense pain through his body. He screamed and crumpled to the floor, curling up into a ball as the blows rained down on him.

After a few seconds, Mackay sensed his assailants' frustration - he was hurting but they were failing to inflict any real damage with their punches. This prompted them to change tack and they began to kick him relentlessly. It was only then that Mackay, for the first time in his life, began to feel frightened - truly terrified. He'd seen that the men were wearing balaclavas. Were they just softening him up before they robbed him, or was it worse? Was this it? Game over?

'What the fuck's this?' screamed a drunken voice in a harsh Edinburgh accent. The kicking stopped and Mackay caught a glimpse of Big Rab Anderson out of the corner of his eye. Anderson was naked save for his saltire boxer shorts, over which spilled an enormous belly, which wobbled with an indented ripple. Anderson was fiery at the best of times, but, in a situation like this, and booze fuelled, he was incandescent with rage.

The bloodlust in his bleary red eyes wasn't lost on the two assailants, who crucially hesitated to face the onslaught from their flank. Mackay was glad he'd left his golf clubs propped against the banister at the foot of the stairs, as he saw his nine iron crash into the balaclava of the leading intruder with a soft thud. The stroke would have hooked the ball out of bounds on the first at Royal Burgess, no doubt eliciting a ripple of laughter from the more observant members sitting in the clubhouse.

However, undeterred, Anderson played his second more like a bunker shot, catching the intruder under the chin with an almighty thwack as he followed through.

As a contest, the encounter was over and the intruders began to edge back towards the door, continually parrying blows from the flailing nine iron as they retreated. Mackay got to his feet and positioned himself off Anderson's shoulder, taking care to avoid the back swing from the nine iron. Mackay ached all over and he was badly bruised, but he sensed that nothing was seriously wrong with him.

Mackay watched as the leading intruder managed to get both hands around the face of the club, nullifying its offensive capability, but this allowed Anderson to control the upper part of the staff with his right hand, using his left fist to smash into the man's unprotected face. The man's head snapped backwards and he semi-pirouetted into his colleague, who bundled him out into the street.

By the time Anderson reached the outside step, they were out of sight. As he stood framed by the open door, Mackay could see that his back was wet with sweat. Anderson turned to face Mackay and discharged a couple of boar-like snorts before slamming the door shut. Then he flung the nine iron on the floor and plunged onto the sofa, exhausted.

Mackay saw that his briefcase containing Steadman's notebook had gone.

'Well, that's one way,' Anderson paused to exhale loudly, 'of sobering up.' He breathed out again. There was silence as the two Scotsmen turned over the whole unpleasant experience in their minds.

It was Anderson who spoke first. 'Who the hell were they?'

'Fuck knows,' replied Mackay, dwelling on what might have been if the fat oaf on the sofa next to him hadn't been at a conference in London that day. He thought about his attackers. Were they two desperate drug addicts intent on robbery, or was this Craven trying to get Steadman's notebook back?

'Anything broken?' asked Anderson, trying to sound compassionate.

'Just a few bruises.'

Anderson wiped sweat from his brow. 'Listen, I know the police have given up on muggings and robbery in this shite city, but that was serious. Those guys need to be locked up.'

'Yes, they were violent,' agreed Mackay.

'I think you should call the rozzers.'

Mackay nodded and walked slowly through to the kitchen, gingerly testing his sore muscles. He returned with two cold lagers and sat next to Anderson on the sofa.

'This might not be robbers.'

Anderson finished his lager in a oner. 'Not robbers? What then?'

Mackay told him of his suspicions about Craven, Platt's death, Bridger's near admission of guilt, and the scandal involving the Atlantic and General Trading Company. Anderson sat still and silent throughout, snorting occasionally, gulping his second lager, not interrupting. After he'd finished, Mackay paused, rubbing his neck where the most painful blow had fallen. 'Well, what do you think?'

Anderson hesitated before answering, his face knotted together as if contemplating some complex theorem. Finally, he turned on the sofa to face Mackay. 'Sounds like bollocks to me. You always were a fantasist, Tom. It's all too incredible to be true – it's just a series of big coincidences.'

Mackay was disappointed. 'You're probably right, Rab. Whether Craven's involved or not is really irrelevant. That was scary.' Mackay paused. 'Shall I call Inspector Woodhouse or the local police?'

'I would call Woodhouse,' replied Rab. 'You'll get a better response from him if he thinks it's linked to this Caspian business.'

Mackay nodded his agreement with this advice. He picked up his wallet from the mantelpiece. If his attackers *had* been robbers, he thought, surely they would have taken the wallet. He found Inspector Woodhouse's card and called the number on it.

'Can I speak to Inspector Woodhouse please...? Would you mind asking him to call Tom Mackay when he gets in...yes, he knows what it's about.' Mackay put the phone down and returned to the sofa.

'Right. I'm off for a shower,' said Anderson. 'Got to look my best for the fleshpots of the capital.'

Anderson left the room and Mackay reached for the remote control. He switched on Channel 4 News and saw pictures of the prime minister being pelted with eggs during a visit to Stevenage. The mob was more aggressive than the one Mackay had seen outside Clapham Junction earlier, except this time the skirmish was more even, because Mr Major's special branch officers were more experienced at keeping away the determined activists trying to get close to him. The phone rang and Mackay picked it up.

'Tom Mackay?' said a voice smoothly.

'Yes.'

'Alex Williams.' The caller needed no further introduction - he was the senior partner of Blake and Lander. 'Tom, I'll come straight to the point. I understand one or two issues have arisen on the audit you're currently undertaking - Caspian Credit - would I be right?'

'That's right, Alex,' replied Mackay, as evenly as he could manage.

'I'd like to offer you my help.' The senior partner adjusted his tone from smooth to velvety. 'Would you like me to help you, Tom?'

'Yes, I would.'

'That's excellent. Why don't you come and see me first thing tomorrow morning, say 8.30? Do you know where my office is?'

'I do, yes.' Mackay heard other voices whispering at Williams's end of the line.

The senior partner continued in the same warm tone. 'If I'm to help you, Tom, it's best not to involve any external parties at this stage. Keep it all intra-firm for now, until we decide what's best to do.' He hesitated. 'Don't you agree?'

Mackay wasn't surprised at Williams's request. 'Yes, if you think that's best, Alex.'

'I do, Tom, I do.' Williams paused. 'In fact, Tom, I wouldn't even mention our meeting to Silas Craven for the moment – let's see where we all stand before we bring him in, shall we?'

That's interesting, thought Mackay. 'OK, Alex.'

'Fine, tomorrow at 8.30 then.' Before Mackay could respond, Williams had hung up.

Mackay went to the fridge and got another lager. He returned to the lounge and sat down on the sofa. How had Williams found out about Caspian? Would they throw him to the wolves or were they after Craven?

It was significant that Craven hadn't been invited. It was well known that, following the bitter succession battle, there was no love lost between Williams and Craven, but surely Williams couldn't cut Craven loose. Craven knew where too many of the bodies were buried. There was no doubt now that the £7 million insurance fraud was genuine, but how far did it go? Murder?

Mackay was still puzzling over how Williams had managed to unearth Caspian when the phone rang for a second time.

'Tom Mackay?' asked the caller.

What now? thought Mackay. I can't take much more of this stress. 'Yes,' he answered apprehensively.

'It's Inspector Woodhouse, Tom – you left a message for me earlier.'

'Er, yes, Inspector,' spluttered Mackay with relief, using a mouthful of beer to buy time while he considered what he was going to say. Since the call from Williams, Mackay had cooled on sharing his experiences of the last hour with the policeman, and he'd also decided against telling the inspector his conspiracy theories, at least until he'd had a chance to meet with Williams.

'Have I caught you in the middle of your supper?'

'No, just an early beer,' replied Mackay, loudly clearing his throat. What could he say?

'What is it then?' asked Woodhouse.

'Not much I'm afraid, probably not important, just something that one of the girls in the office said.'

'Who in the office?' pressed Woodhouse.

Mackay thought quickly. 'Sally Purcell.'

Woodhouse hesitated as if processing something in his mind. 'Yes, go on.'

'Well, she said that Keith had told her something was odd with the Caspian audit.' Mackay immediately regretted using the word odd and attempted to backtrack. 'When I say odd, what I mean is an unresolved audit issue.'

'I see. Have you found anything *odd* yourself, sir?'

Mackay found the sarcastic tone in Woodhouse's voice alarming. 'No,' he said robustly, but then added, 'but I haven't finished the audit yet.' Mackay sensed it was best to be vague until after tomorrow's meeting with Williams.

'Do you know Sally Purcell well, Mr Mackay?' said Woodhouse pointedly.

Now Mackay was concerned. 'Yes, we're good friends, Inspector.'

'Good friends eh? Were you screwing her before Keith Platt's death, sir?' asked the inspector, making the question sound criminal, sordid and condemning.

The accusation caught Mackay by surprise and threw him off balance. 'No I was not,' stammered Mackay. 'Look, what is this, Woodhouse?'

The policeman didn't answer the question, but instead asked another question of his own. 'Where were you yesterday evening, sir?' Again it was the 'sir' part of the question that alarmed Mackay the most – the policeman had always called him Mr Mackay or Tom, never sir, and the use of the word concerned him.

'I was at a Tory Party meeting in Putney,' said Mackay quickly.

'Many people there, sir?'

Mackay felt on firmer ground. 'At least a dozen. Commander Roper, he's the agent, he'll confirm it.' Mackay pressed his ear against the phone – was he on a loudspeaker? 'What is this, Inspector?'

Woodhouse's voice was cold. 'Your client, Jonathan Bridger, died last night.'

Mackay was stunned – surely this *was* foul play. He glanced at his front door to make sure it was locked. 'How?' he said weakly.

'Problem with his gas fire. He was well into his second bottle of Scotch so I doubt if he knew much about it. Seems the flame blew out – it was lucky there wasn't an explosion.'

Mackay imagined Bridger slumped on his sofa in a drunken stupor, oblivious to Craven hovering over the gas fire, switching the tap off, waiting for the flame to die, then turning it on.

'You see my dilemma, Mr Mackay,' continued the inspector evenly. 'Too many coincidences here for me. My boss, on the other hand, she's the department's budget-holder, and she's a more favourable view of coincidences than me – a hit-and-run driver, a domestic accident, it happens all the time, but to two connected individuals within a month? I don't buy it, and I warn you now, and this is the only warning you'll get from me, if I find out you've held anything back, anything at all, I'll be after you, and I won't let go. I don't like threatening decent professional folk like yourself, but sometimes it's necessary.' Mackay suspected the opposite was true but he decided against debating the point. 'Is there anything you'd like to add to what you've just told me, Tom?'

'No,' replied Mackay resolutely.

'OK then, sir. I'd be obliged if you would stay in London until further notice. No more dirty weekends in Gibraltar without my permission.'

Woodhouse hung up before he could reply. Mackay wasn't sure whether he was shocked more by the news of Bridger's death, or by the fact that Woodhouse knew he'd been to Gibraltar with Sally. He instantly regretted not coming clean with the policeman. The situation was getting out of control and Woodhouse could protect him. Sure, tomorrow's meeting with Williams might be to his advantage, but he was convinced now that these deaths weren't coincidences.

He heard Rab come out of the shower upstairs and head for the guest bedroom. One thing was certain – Mackay wouldn't be leaving the side of that fearsome warrior this evening.

CHAPTER SIXTEEN

Thursday 1 May 1997 – Election Day

DON'T GIVE UP ON US, SAYS MAJOR
BLAIR GIVES HIS ALL ON THE LAST DAY OF THE CAMPAIGN
OUR KIND OF GUY, SINATRA IS, SAYS CONGRESS

Despite his earlier promise to himself, Mackay left Rab at midnight and travelled back to Putney alone. He'd seen that the West End was busier than usual and mobbed with City traders having a last drink under the *ancien regime*. During the evening, Rab had pursued a Kiwi nightmare named Rebecca, and, while Mackay had been prepared to provide some support as wingman, his main priority was to stay fresh and alert for his meeting with Williams.

Consequently, he was up first and out of the flat before anyone else had stirred. He had a smooth commute into the City and was at No. 1 Westmorland Park by 8.15. The building was the grandest of the four sites the firm had in London, befitting the distinguished senior accountants who inhabited the luxurious recesses of its upper floors.

Mackay had been in the building once before but only to attend a presentation on the ground floor. He couldn't find the lifts and was soon wandering through semi-dark kitchens in the basement, where, while fumbling for a light switch, he knocked into a heavily laden hostess trolley, sending a variety of plates and cutlery crashing noisily onto the tiled floor. One of the security guards appeared from nowhere and directed him to a dimly lit bay where the service lift was hidden. No wonder I couldn't find these, thought Mackay, as he got in and pressed the button for the seventh floor.

The lift door opened onto a screened ante-room. Mackay walked through the ante-room and into a reception area, where he noticed the main lifts. There was a library-like hush on the floor and a sweet smell of flowers - possibly the real thing, thought Mackay. A second sniff, however, suggested chemicals and an expensive plug-in.

If the firm's interior designers had intended to recreate a sumptuous Edwardian meet and greet area, they had succeeded - the ornate wood panelling was exquisitely carved, the plush mauve carpet was thick pile, and the glittering chandeliers were pure Titanic. In the midst of it all sat a gorgeous, blue-eyed blonde.

She'd noticed Mackay's arrival by the service lift, so her smile was not the one she gave to visiting captains of industry. What she was doing manning the seventh-floor reception desk of Blake and Lander was beyond him: here was a girl who should be on a catwalk. After a few seconds of wordless flapping, Mackay managed to blurt out, 'Alex Williams, please.'

She smiled at him again and gestured towards a green leather sofa, which sat under huge Victorian photographs of Mr Blake and Mr Lander.

Mackay sat down and picked up a copy of the Financial Times, which lay on a table adjacent to the sofa. May as well look keen, he thought, as he stole a furtive glance at the receptionist. She was at right angles to him now, and he saw a slender white arm appear from under the desk and reach for the phone.

'Tom Mackay to see you,' she chirped sweetly. There was a muffled reply from the other end and she replaced the handset on the cradle.

Mackay flicked through the Financial Times, looking at the pictures. It was hot and the paper began to have a hypnotic effect on him. Because of last night's beers he started to feel drowsy. He drifted into a trance-like state featuring the attractive receptionist.

The sound of a heavy door opening jolted him into full consciousness and he sprang to his feet, sending the Financial Times cart wheeling to the floor. He looked up and the receptionist smiled at him like he was the village idiot. He stooped to pick up the newspaper, unable to shake Alex Williams's hand when he straightened up. The senior partner stood motionless as Mackay awkwardly transferred the newspaper to his left hand, freeing up his right for the handshake. Williams's grip was odd – was it Masonic?

'Thanks very much for coming to see me at such short notice, Tom. Shall we go into my office?'

Mackay followed the king of the firm through the oak doors into the throne room and was impressed with what he saw. Williams's desk was framed by a huge floor-to-ceiling window, through which Mackay could see the grey brown water of the Thames and London Bridge in the distance. In stark contrast to the windowless 'Edwardian' reception, this room was filled with natural light and was airy and modern. There was a large mahogany table at the far end of the room, at which sat four grey-haired courtiers. A fifth man – who was about Mackay's age – sat at the end of the table with an open notebook in front of him, pen poised.

Williams headed for the chair at the far end of the table and invited Mackay to sit next to him. Mackay took the chair, clasped his hands together, and sat back. If the Gestapo-like positioning of Williams and his courtiers had been intended to intimidate him, it had failed. Mackay felt unusually relaxed and under-awed by the situation – strangely at ease with himself.

Mackay looked more closely at Williams and saw one of those square, pugnacious, stocky types, balding but trim looking, more nightclub bruiser than accountant – his manner an unstable blend of affability and menace. Yesterday, Mackay would have been fearful, but, after last night's encounter with the thugs, he didn't care.

Williams looked at him without seeing him. Mackay was merely a minor ailment that needed treatment. The medication would be a simple dose of money, a promotion and the raising of career expectations, balanced with threats of the sack and litigation. Every man had his price, and Williams suspected that this man's price wouldn't be high, although Mackay's careless body language and lack of deference began to concern him. Indeed, the man before Williams was *so* self-assured that the senior partner was tempted to drop the agreed strategy and adopt a more conciliatory tactic from the outset. A loud yawn from Mackay convinced him of this, so Williams sat back in his chair and threw his hands around his head.

'Are we keeping you up, Tom?' asked Williams.

'Sorry, Alex,' replied Mackay, 'late night on the stump.' Out of his peripheral vision Mackay noticed the four courtiers follow Williams's lead and simultaneously recline. The manoeuvre was embarrassing for all concerned and reminded Mackay of the Siamese children in the King and I. Mackay stifled a smirk.

Williams looked away from his courtiers as he continued. 'Yes, I understand you've been helping get our own Silas Craven elected,' said Williams, glad he'd been handed an easy lead into the purpose of the meeting.

'That's right,' replied Mackay. 'The seat's been Tory since 1905, so it shouldn't be difficult.'

'Excellent. Excellent.' The senior partner brought his hands from behind his head and leaned forwards slightly in his chair. Mackay glanced to his right but there was no response from the courtiers and they remained fully reclined. The fifth man put his pen to his notebook and Mackay sensed that the exchange of pleasantries was over.

'Well, you know why I've asked you here, Tom,' began Williams softly. 'Perhaps you could tell us in your own words what's been going on at Caspian. Please speak freely – we're all colleagues here.'

Mackay doubted whether they *were* all on the same team and he regretted not having an ally with him, but, despite this, he gave the room a full report of the Caspian audit – his views, opinions and suspicions. He set out his thoughts on Bridger's death, inducing a bout of fidgeting amongst the courtiers, despite Mackay qualifying what he said with caveats about evidence.

During the course of his diatribe, Mackay sensed that Williams already knew much of what he said. Each piece of information elicited a grimace from the senior partner, whose screwed-up face gradually contorted into some sort of fleshy Kleenex. Mackay sensed that Williams's earlier geniality was gone and that the bruiser would soon lash out at the nearest target.

Years of practice, however, had taught Williams how to control his emotions, so, when he continued, his voice was calm and even. 'As you say, Tom, no hard evidence and a lot of speculation on your part. Serious allegations these – allegations against a senior figure in this firm and a respected member of the financial community. For fuck's sake, this time tomorrow the man will be an MP.' Williams flicked open a slim paper folder on his desk in front of him. Mackay could see it was his own personnel file.

'The thing is what to do, Tom? For a start, it's possible that investing the insurance rebate in property was authorised by senior management at the bank. In fact, that very thing has been confirmed to me by the bank themselves. It's difficult to see how fraud has been committed in those circumstances.'

Clever, thought Mackay. With Bridger gone, there was nothing to contradict such an assertion.

'I can see how it would have been easy to miss this,' continued Williams gently. 'You clearly weren't aware that the documentation supporting this transaction was held at group. I'm sure most of us would have failed to spot it.' Williams smiled at him in an understanding way, but the threat of negligence was clear. 'The three deaths you've mentioned, Tom – Vassallo, Platt, Bridger – one a drunken suicide, another a hit-and-run and the third a gas leak. All tenuously linked, yes, but over a period of thirty years, and each murdered by Silas Craven. It's preposterous. I've known the man for twenty-five years myself.'

'There's the journalist as well,' volunteered Mackay.

Williams frowned. 'He'll turn up. He hasn't even been reported missing, has he?'

It was clear Williams intended to bury the whole Caspian stench down a 300-foot concrete-lined silo. The only outstanding issue was

Mackay - would he scurry in behind the rapidly closing ranks of the firm, or squeal to Inspector Woodhouse?

'Now, Tom, I really value the work you've done on this job. It's been difficult. Senior staff have departed from our procedures, guidelines haven't been followed, misjudgements have been made.' Williams paused. 'Do you know what this is?'

'It looks like my personnel file.'

'It is. It is. To be frank, Tom, it's not stellar, is it?'

'No. I haven't felt particularly challenged in recent years, Alex,' replied Mackay with a touch of sarcasm. He saw Williams try to hide his irritation.

'No. Well, as I said, Tom, you've done well on this job - very well. So well in fact that I think you're ready for more responsibility. How about promotion with immediate effect - a battlefield promotion as it were?'

Williams glanced at Mackay to gauge his reaction but Mackay sat impassively. The senior partner continued, 'Of course, there's the issue of your bonuses. I see from here that you've never had one, despite being eligible for the last four years. I'm sure we can see our way to putting that right and backdating this year's to '93. That would add up to a tidy sum.'

Mackay had done the maths before Williams had finished speaking - it was forty-eight grand. Mackay could see that Williams didn't find negotiating with him demeaning in any way. To him, Mackay merely represented a problem that needed to be solved. This was just business.

Mackay was pleased with the generosity of the pay-off but surprised when Williams went further. 'Of course, individuals like you, Tom, who show exceptional loyalty to Blake and Lander, can, in time, be expected to reach the very highest levels of the firm.'

Mackay looked at the courtiers and imagined himself joining their ranks. He began to realise that he had a stronger hand than he'd thought, so he decided to chance his arm. 'That would depend on what "in time" meant, Alex.'

'Four, five years at the most. Certainly on my watch anyway. Of course, further progression would depend on your absolute commitment to the firm, Tom.' Williams paused. 'Do I have your absolute commitment to the firm?'

'I am committed,' replied Mackay, as if swearing an oath to some ancient Masonic sect.

'Oh, that is good,' said Williams, giving him the same plastic smile that Craven used. Did the firm purchase plastic smiles wholesale wondered Mackay?

Mackay half-expected applause from the courtiers but instead they stood up when Williams did and advanced to shake Mackay's hand. After a minute of meaningless small talk, Williams took Mackay by the arm and guided him to the heavy oak doors. As Williams put his hand on the shiny brass handle and opened the door, he turned to Mackay. 'I do appreciate your candour and commitment, Tom. You leave the Caspian loose ends to me.'

Williams reached into his jacket pocket and brought out a silver card holder. 'Any problems, any problems at all, please call me directly on this number. I'll see that Jane puts you straight through.'

Mackay couldn't help giving a deferential nod as he turned to head for the lifts, before realising that Williams was holding onto his arm. The senior partner casually tightened his grip and brought his face six inches from Mackay's. Mackay could smell coffee on his breath.

Williams glanced at the iconic pictures of Mr Blake and Mr Lander and squeezed hard. The menace in his voice was clear. 'This firm's been operating for over 120 years now, Tom. It's a great firm, an institution in fact, and nothing, but nothing, is going to jeopardise its future. Not on my watch, not on anybody's watch. Do I make myself clear?'

Mackay was shocked in the face of Williams's bare aggression. 'I understand, Alex,' he replied, as resolutely as he could manage. 'I fully understand.'

'Excellent,' he said, releasing both his grip and his intimidating stare, 'that's excellent.' Williams spun round and returned to his office.

Mackay stole one last glance at the attractive receptionist, then headed for the lifts.

CHAPTER SEVENTEEN

Thursday 1 May 1997 – the same day

From the corner of the sixth-floor juniors' room in Wessex Court, Craven had a view across the road to the office of the senior partner at Westmorland Park. Craven had stood in the empty room for some time, watching, watching, until he saw Mackay come out of the door and cross the road.

Craven shrank into the wall as he saw Mackay walk stiffly towards him then disappear through the door below. Mackay was clearly in pain – Craven regretted that last night's attempt to scare him had got out of hand. Craven heard the phone ring in his office across the corridor and ran to get it.

It was Alex Williams. 'Silas.'

'Yes.'

'He's taken it,' Williams said coldly.

Craven was relieved. 'Good…and the bank?'

Williams continued in the same detached tone. 'They're on board. The CEO is a member of my club. He's got someone at Group to sign off on a document authorising a loan to Bridger for the seven million. The same document also instructs Bridger to invest the balance of the seven million offshore.'

'Will it wash?' asked Craven apprehensively.

'It's hardly material, is it? And who's going to spot it? We're the auditors, aren't we? Williams paused, allowing his tone to switch from detached to fierce.

'Now you listen to me Silas. Mackay made some serious allegations about you in here. You keep a lid on them, do you understand me? If I hear anything else about this it'll be you who falls off a rock.'

'That was an accident,' replied Craven weakly.

'DO YOU UNDERSTAND ME?' bellowed Williams.

'Yes,' said Craven, but Williams had already hung up.

Four floors below Craven, Mackay sat at his desk, aimlessly flicking through a file, too excited to concentrate.

Tony King, seeing Mackay's lack of productivity, felt obliged to comment. 'You busy then?'

'You know me, Tony, continually generating fees for the firm. I'm a money machine, I am.'

'Certainly looks that way,' said King sarcastically.

Mackay was mildly irritated. He looked up from his desk. He couldn't resist it. 'Bet you a hundred quid I'm promoted before you.'

King snorted in surprise. Staff weren't told about promotions until August and it was common knowledge that he was next in line after Platt. With Platt gone, King's promotion was a certainty. What was Mackay thinking of? He wasn't even in the running.

'Try 200,' said King.

Mackay got up from his desk, stood opposite King and shook his hand. 'You're on.'

An easy 200 quid, thought Mackay. Then it struck him that a benefit of his promotion would be a move into his own office at the senior end of the building, which would mean, sadly, an end to his cohabitation with King.

Given that Mackay's new patron was none other than the senior partner, he felt immune from departmental authority and disinclined to do much work. He felt a sense of liberation and celebration, so decided to go to the pub for an early lunch.

The pub was packed with the bedrock of the outgoing government - City traders, investment bankers and fund managers – all drowning their sorrows and clinging to the hope of a ballot box miracle. Well-heeled corporate lawyers jostled with fat tax advisors for space at the bar, while a dozen Basildon men crowded noisily around a fruit machine in the corner, swigging lager out of branded bottles with every spin of the wheels. Mackay spotted some Blake and Lander journeymen seated on the dais at the far end of the pub, so he joined them.

By the time he lurched back to his office three hours later, it was clear his liquid lunch had rendered him incapable of any meaningful bean counting. He decided to call it a day and clear his desk, which he did by opening the large drawer at the bottom and sweeping everything into it using the full length of his arm. He kicked the drawer closed and grabbed forcefully at his jacket, a quiet ripping sound indicating he'd failed to unhook it properly before pulling.

As Mackay approached the door on his way out of his office, Tony King appeared carrying a vending cup. Mackay swerved to miss him but drunkenly overcorrected to avoid a bin, catching King on the elbow. The contents of the cup sprayed in a 270° arc, drenching King and leaving a large orange stain over his shirt and groin. A scan of Mackay's own suit revealed he'd found the only dry quadrant. When King realised this, it intensified his rage, and he flung the empty soup cup at Mackay's back as he left the room. The cup missed and hit the cream wall on the other side of the corridor, creating an orange polka-dot effect worthy of Laurence Llewellyn Bowen.

'Sorry, Tony.'

'You clumsy twat,' shouted King, but Mackay was already safely in the lift.

Mackay decided to take the train rather than the tube, hoping the walk to Waterloo would sober him up. Although he did feel fresher as he boarded, the carriage was hot and, by Clapham Junction, he'd dozed off, waking only when the train terminated at Richmond.

By the time he'd caught another train back to Putney and walked to the flat, it had gone five o'clock. A further short nap and a lukewarm shower completed his sobering-up process, and, after changing into his election uniform, he headed for Balfour Street.

It was a warm, pleasant evening and the sight of Roper fidgeting nervously outside the office couldn't detract from it. Mackay noticed that all the windows on the second-floor flat now displayed large, bright, 'Vote Labour' posters, whereas the blue flaming torch on the ground floor was dog eared and faded.

'Lovely evening, Lawrence,' beamed Mackay.

'Make the most of it, Tom,' said Roper. 'The sun won't shine again under Labour.'

Mackay smiled at the weak joke. 'Do I finally detect a note of defeatism?'

'Just reality. We'll be alright here of course, but the exit polls from the marginals aren't good.' Roper paused. 'I won't stay in the UK you know.'

'The holiday home in Madeira?' asked Mackay.

'Not big enough. I'll sell up here and buy something bigger on the island. The market's probably peaked here anyway - I can't see people wanting to invest in UK property when they've got rubbish and dead folk piling up on their doorsteps.'

'Mmm...' mused Mackay, not convinced by the reference to the Winter of Discontent. 'I'll be off as well if it gets that bad. There's no end of secondment opportunities in Australia.'

'But you can't leave, Tom,' said Roper energetically. 'Someone needs to keep the flame burning. It's time the younger generation took over from old farts like me.' He paused. 'Here's a thought - why don't you take over from me, as agent I mean. You know Silas, you're good with people, you've got more of a lateral view than most of the automatons who work here - then, when Silas retires, you'd be in pole position to take over.'

Mackay was surprised. 'Well, I'm flattered, Lawrence.'

Mackay realised that, from an external point of view, his relationship with Craven must look good - Roper had no idea he suspected him of murder. Mackay was saved from further unexpected and unwarranted praise by Annabel, who appeared at the door in a blue 'Vote Craven' polo shirt.

'Silas is on his way, Commander,' she said.

'Roger that,' said Roper, snapping back into military mode. 'Let's head over to the recreation centre.'

'Anything more for me to do, Lawrence?' asked Mackay. 'I'll be there for the declaration, of course, only I've got a date.' The question was directed at Roper but intended for Annabel. Mackay saw her flinch slightly and, when she spoke, her voice lacked its usual careless confidence.

'Tommy's got a date,' she said. 'Anybody we know?'

'A girl from the office. I'll bring her along tonight.'

'Does she bat for us?' asked Roper.

'No,' replied Mackay. 'She's an American.'

'Well, bring her along to our...er...celebrations – it'd be good to meet her. I think the declaration will be about one-ish.'

Roper turned and went back into the building. Before following him, Annabel caught Mackay's eye. She looked at him for a couple of seconds, her mouth slightly open, then tightened her lips as if to speak but instead exhaled heavily through her nose before leaving. Always the way with women, thought Mackay – as soon as you were off the market they were interested.

He wondered whether his relationship with Sally was informal enough to allow further exploration of this first sign of interest from Annabel. Could this be achieved during a vague and lengthy overlap period? The idea was appealing and pleasurable, and images of breakfast with Sally followed by evening cocoa with Annabel filled his mind.

He was surprised that, when he sat down at Sally's table in the wine bar shortly afterwards, he could still only see Annabel. Was his libido trying to tell him something? Sally was dressed in a blue business suit with a white shirt wide open at the neck – she looked great. She gave him a hard look and he noticed that she'd almost finished a large glass of Chardonnay.

'Where've you been?' she asked curtly, as if she could read his thoughts about Annabel.

'I'm not late, am I?'

'You know I don't like to be kept waiting.'

He tried to lighten the mood. 'I had important party business to take care of – my country needs me.'

'Get me another drink,' she drawled in the American twang he loved.

Mackay walked to the bar and ordered a large white wine, and, as there was no draught bitter, a bottle of Becks. He returned to the table, where he sensed a thaw.

'Show me your bruises then,' she said, in a conciliatory tone.

He lifted his shirt to parade the purplest one under his rib cage.

She jabbed it with her finger and he flinched in pain. 'Bloody hell, Sal!'

'Certainly looks painful,' she said, attempting a second jab. Mackay caught her finger and held it tightly. 'Well, what are we going to do about Silas, Tom?' she asked, distracting him long enough to free her finger.

Mackay spoke robotically. 'Do? We're going to do nothing. Williams will have told Silas by now that I've been bought off. Silas will call off his thugs, he'll get elected, I'll be promoted and get a bonus, the good name of Blake and Lander won't be dragged through the mud, the merger between Southern and Caledonian will be a success, and…' He paused. '…I get the girl.'

She frowned. 'And Keith and Bridger, and that journalist. What about them?'

'Nick Steadman will turn up. The others were suicide and a hit-and-run.'

She took a large gulp out of her glass and he drained the rest of his bottle. 'Very neat and tidy,' she said sarcastically.

'It is if you take the Mackay view,' he said, slightly slurring his words. 'I'm a company man now, you know.' The strong lager had reacted with the latent alcohol from lunch and he suddenly felt quite drunk.

'Listen, Sal, why don't we get a takeaway pizza and head back to the flat. Nothing's going to happen until the early hours and we could catch the start of the election coverage on the telly.'

She glanced over to the group of teenagers in the corner, who were becoming increasingly boisterous with every mouthful of Hooch. They had been amusing to begin with, but now they were irritating. 'OK,' she said, 'this bar's not what it was. Let's be adults and go watch politics.'

'Great,' said Mackay, getting to his feet, his mind dwelling on other adult activities that could only be pursued at home.

Of the two Dimbleby brothers, Mackay found David the more tolerable, so they watched the BBC. It was fortunate for Dimbleby that the TV in Mackay's flat was not two way, as the great broadcaster would've been distracted from describing each New Labour gain by the X-rated display taking place on the sofa a few feet from his flickering face.

Mackay found it difficult to concentrate on anything other than the matter in hand, but, when he heard Dimbleby describe the loss of Birmingham Edgbaston and then Crosby with an eighteen per cent swing to Labour, he looked up.

'Bloody hell - this is a meltdown. We haven't won a seat yet - even Craven could be in trouble.'

'For God's sake, Tom, switch that off and please finish what you're doing.'

The five-a-side football hall at the Heath Recreation Centre was as full as it had been the night of 'Question Time', although now the seats in which the general public had sat were replaced with long tables where tellers perched, counting voting papers. Rather than noise, there was an excitable buzz around the hall, with the only distinguishable voice that of Roper.

Mackay had known as soon as they'd arrived that opening the second bottle of Chardonnay had been a mistake - the occasion demanded a degree of gravitas, which both he and Sally were now incapable of.

Mackay tried to look serious as Geoff bounded up to him, his blue rosette spinning round like a half-drunken propeller. 'It's bad, Tom – that's their pile and that's ours.'

Mackay looked across the room at the two even piles of ballot papers. If anything, the pile on the left looked slightly larger. 'Which one's ours?' he asked.

'The one on the right,' replied Geoff.

Sally shuffled her feet, impatient to be introduced. 'Geoff, this is Sally Purcell, a close friend of mine.'

'Nice to meet you, Sally,' he said automatically. 'Sorry, must dash.' He bounded off towards Roper.

'Clearly an important man,' giggled Sally.

Mackay nodded. 'Our Geoff doesn't get out much – this result means a lot to him.'

Mackay could see Craven at the far end of the hall by the edge of a platform where he assumed the declaration would take place. Craven stood motionless, high above Roper – almost deity-like – while Annabel and the other party workers busied themselves around him like disciples.

Craven caught Mackay's eye and acknowledged him with a lazy flicker of his eyelid. To Craven's left, a fat balding man, who Mackay remembered as the Labour candidate, Paul Smith, was locked in conversation with Roger Metcalfe. Behind them was the Liberal Democrat candidate, who did nothing but smile, and, to his right, was the returning officer, who began tapping on the microphone in the middle of the platform.

After completing his sound check, the returning officer straightened up and cleared his throat. 'Er...hello everyone, we're just about to finish the count. I'll give the result in five to ten minutes.'

The announcement made little impact on the Liberal, UKIP or Green candidates – they were also rans – but Mackay saw the Labour candidate Paul Smith fiddle with his red rosette, and even Craven looked nervous.

Ten long minutes passed. Mackay saw the returning officer consult, then re-consult, with his staff, then consult again. A few more papers were added to Smith's pile and then to Craven's, then Smith's. All of the candidates drifted towards the platform.

Sally touched Mackay's arm. 'Shall we join your colleagues?'

'No, let's watch from here.' He paused. 'Isn't democracy wonderful?'

'I must say the candidates are very representative,' she said sarcastically. 'Five white, middle-aged men.'

'You'll be in favour of quotas, of course. All-women shortlists I mean.'

She nodded. 'I might be if this is typical of most constituencies here.'

'Please remind me the last time there wasn't a white, middle-aged man in the White House.'

She paused to think. '1989. No one would describe Reagan as middle aged – but yes, I take your point.'

She looked away from him as the returning officer opened his hand and indicated that the candidates should join him on the platform. They filed past him and stood facing the hall. All of them, except the Liberal Democrat candidate, who continued to smile, looked very serious. A hush fell in the hall as the returning officer began to speak.

'I, Richard Mead, being the returning officer for the Barnes and West Putney constituency, declare that the votes cast in the general election in the said constituency are as follows: Christopher Bryant, UK Independence Party, one thousand seven hundred and six, Silas Craven, Conservative Party, twenty thousand four hundred and twelve, Colin Finch, Liberal Democrat, three thousand and twenty-six, Jonathan Pardoe, Green Party, nine hundred and sixty-seven.'

Mead paused theatrically, fiddled with the microphone, and cleared his throat. There was an impatient shuffling in the hall and a roar erupted from the Labour supporters around Smith. 'Paul Smith...' began Mead, but he had missed his chance and was drowned out by the escalating din filling the hall. 'Paul Smith, the Labour Party candidate...' but his voice was lost in the noise, as the Labour supporters started chanting. All that could be hear above the clamour was... 'Smithyeee...Smithyeee...Smithyeee...Smithyeee...Smithyeee...Smithyee...'

'Quiet please,' cajoled Mead. 'Paul Smith, the Labour Party candidate, twenty thousand...' The chanting intensified but Mead decided to battle on, 'twenty thousand, three hundred...'

Mackay saw Craven fling his arms up as Roper and Annabel took off and hugged each other mid-air. There was a stunned silence from the Labour ranks and Paul Smith looked more crumpled than usual.

Mead hadn't finished. 'Twenty thousand, three hundred and forty-four, and I hereby declare that Silas Anthony Craven has been duly elected to represent the parliamentary constituency of Barnes and West Putney.'

Roper began a round of thin applause, which died down as Craven approached the microphone. Craven's smile was fixed and his tone velvety. 'I'd like to thank the police, my agent and his staff...'

'I can't listen to this,' said Mackay.

'Hardly a cause for celebration, is it?' declared Sally. 'A majority of eleven thousand down to a hundred.'

'No, Sal, it isn't. Let's go before we have to say something nice to the new representative of the people.'

She took his hand and led him out of the hall. The reality of Craven's win slowly began to sink in. Surely there were supposed to be safeguards in the system to weed out those who weren't fit for office. Mackay thought back to the succession of reprobates who'd reached ministerial rank in the Major government and realised that any safeguards that did exist were at best weak.

New Labour would, eventually, end up the same. Mackay reflected on who New Labour were - were they just a collection of self-serving lawyers, media-savvy journalists and time-served over-promoted union officials? It was difficult to know what they actually stood for and it seemed to him that they'd been elected simply because they weren't the Tories. The age of the professional politician had certainly arrived. Britain had been booming under the Tories. Odd thing, democracy, thought Mackay.

CHAPTER EIGHTEEN

Friday 2 May 1997

LABOUR LANDSLIDE
PORTILLO, FORSYTH, LANG SWEPT AWAY IN ROUT
SLOWDOWN AS HOUSE PRICES TAKE BREATHER

When he walked into his office the next morning, Mackay saw that there was a yellow post-it note stuck to his computer. It read, 'Tom, please pop up to see me when you get in. Silas.'

As Mackay approached Craven's room on the sixth floor, he caught a glimpse of the same red braces that had acted as a hazard warning the previous month. The half-packed boxes strewn across the room indicated that the new member for Barnes and West Putney had already begun the move to Westminster. Mackay doubted whether Craven would completely sever his links with the firm as that would mean surviving solely on a MP's salary.

Craven heard Mackay clip one of the boxes behind him and he spun round. He smiled at Mackay with his signature emotionless warmth and gestured to him that he should sit down.

'You know I have to share an office with two others at Westminster,' said Craven.

'How ever will you manage?' said Mackay, with unguarded sarcasm.

Craven looked at him sharply, momentarily doubting his loyalty. Mackay thought it prudent to build bridges. 'Will you leave the firm altogether?'

'No. I remain as a consultant. Besides, my overheads are too high – I can't leave the private sector altogether. Wives are expensive, you know.'

Mackay knew that Craven was trying to be light-hearted, trying to be nice to him, but it made both men feel uncomfortable. Mackay realised that he disliked Craven. He hoped he would revert back to his usual default disdain, but instead the parliamentarian continued with the uneasy pleasantness.

'Listen, Tom, I've asked you up here to thank you, to thank you for your support over. . . on…er… well…a number of fronts.'

Interesting way of putting it, thought Mackay. Did 'a number of fronts' translate into relentlessly pounding the streets of Barnes wearing a blue rosette and acting as an unpaid cheerleader for the beleaguered John Major, or did it mean ignoring all manner of criminality, ranging from fraud to murder?

Mackay looked at Craven. He was impossible to read. What was going on behind those grey lifeless eyes? Was Mackay living in a parallel universe to think that this man, this MP, this pillar of the financial community, was somehow involved in murder? Well it *was* incredible.

'You weren't involved in the deaths of Platt and Bridger, were you, Silas?' Mackay paused. 'And your first wife, Penny Gray?'

As a minimum, Mackay expected Craven to look away, or at least shift in his seat or clasp his hands together tightly, but instead he was motionless, his gaze fixed intensely on the bridge of Mackay's nose.

'No.'

Craven had been expecting this question. He'd had time to prepare his answer and his body language for it. He gave nothing away. 'Anything else you'd like to ask me, Tom? Anything else you'd like to get off your chest? I can see you're troubled.'

Mackay was pleased that Craven had reverted to his icy norm – he hadn't liked it when he was being nice. Mackay didn't answer, so Craven continued. 'Alex Williams tells me you've a great future in this firm, Tom. He has plans for you. I always knew you were partnership material – you're a player, you can think laterally, you can see the angles.'

'I'm not like you, Silas.'

'You're more like me than you think,' said Craven coldly.

'Bollocks.'

Craven flinched at this and his mouth hardened. It was time to take Mackay down a peg or two. 'We've a lot in common, Tom – more in common than you think.'

'What do you mean by that?' said Mackay, but he knew where Craven was going.

There was a long pause. Craven deliberately let Mackay stew. 'Sally Purcell, for example.'

'You've slept with her?'

'No, not slept with her, Tom.' Craven smiled broadly then wet his lips with the tip of his tongue. 'Just screwed her in the toilet of a Mayfair hotel.'

Mackay leapt forward and tried to grab Craven's throat, but the MP brought up his knee and Mackay bounced off it, falling backwards towards the door. Mackay sprang for a second assault but a voice from behind checked him.

'I'm sorry, Silas. I'll get some of these boxes moved at once.' It was Craven's secretary. She suddenly sensed that Mackay hadn't tripped over a box and that all was not well. 'Is everything alright?'

Mackay skirted round her and left the room, only pausing to leave the words, 'I'll get you, you fucker,' hanging in the air.

There was no sign of Sally in the department and, following the tomato soup incident, Tony King had avoided conversation with him. By the time Mackay was on the District Line heading west, he'd calmed down enough to gather his thoughts.

To hell with them, thought Mackay, to hell with them all. Three years ago it *had* been the departmental rumour that Sally had disappeared with Craven during the firm's Christmas party at the Dorchester. Nothing had ever been admitted to, and, at the time, Mackay had been envious, but he hadn't cared then. Now, he did. Craven had intended to hurt him and he'd succeeded. Did he think Mackay would take this and roll over – all for some poxy promotion and a £48,000 bonus? Craven had miscalculated and now he would be punished.

Mackay arrived at Caspian House and went straight to the third floor. Outside Bridger's office sat a young woman with the bearing of a temp. Mackay sidled up to her desk and, when she spoke, she confirmed his assumption. 'Mrs Paterson's not in today - she's taken some time off. As you can imagine, she's pretty upset.' She paused. 'I'm Mandy. Are you the auditor?'

'Yes, I'm Tom.'

'I was told to expect you. There's a message for you from Inspector Woodhouse. He said he'll be here at about eleven, and that if you were in, would you mind waiting for him.'

'OK, thanks.'

Mackay went into the boardroom and pulled out the files. He'd half-expected them to have disappeared, or at least to have been tampered with, but they all seemed to be how he'd left them. He marked the incriminating pages with post-its and pulled out the fax from Avon and General. This should be enough for Inspector Woodhouse, he thought.

He called Sally at home and at the office but she seemed to have disappeared. Would she confirm what Craven had said? Mackay knew he wasn't being rational and that he shouldn't care about something that may or may not have happened three years ago - he was simply being primeval. That was what Craven wanted - he'd deliberately acted like a Viking, thinking Mackay wouldn't retaliate, but he was wrong.

Mackay suspected Inspector Woodhouse was keen to get Craven and that, even if nothing stuck, he would enjoy making life difficult for him. All Mackay would do would be to point the policeman in the right direction. Mackay would have to look for another job, but that was no bad thing. At least he would be forced to do something with his life.

The phone rang and Mackay picked it up. 'Is that Tom Mackay?'

The voice was familiar. 'Yes.'

'It's Nick Steadman.'

Mackay was relieved. 'Nick, where the hell have you been?'

'Let's just say I fell off a cliff.'

'Fell off?'

'Well, more barged off by a youth trying to nick my wallet.'

'Oh.' Mackay was disappointed and Steadman could hear it in his voice.

'You thought I'd been pushed off by Craven?' said the journalist.

'The thought had crossed my mind.'

'That's what I thought, Tom, until this lad confessed. He thought he'd killed me but I was just out cold for a few days. My leg's broken but I'll make a full recovery.'

'That's good – you just take it easy.' Mackay paused. 'Thinking aloud, did this lad look anything like Craven?'

Steadman hesitated. 'God. I didn't think of that. Yes, he did.' Mackay heard the receiver thump against the wall as Steadman fed more coins into the payphone slot. 'Yes, he did. That would also explain why his expensive brief turned up so quickly from Newcastle.'

'Now do you think you were pushed off?' asked Mackay.

Steadman paused to think. 'Very difficult to say. You've no idea how strong the wind was. It all happened so quickly. He definitely went for my notebook and sort of shoulder-barged me in the process. I couldn't be certain whether he tried to push me over.'

'It's suspicious nevertheless.' Mackay changed the subject. 'Craven won the seat.'

'I know, I've spoken to Roger Metcalfe. Roger's been leant on from above and I've to stop digging. There's no hard evidence against Craven anyway.'

Mackay looked at the file in front of him and was tempted to contradict the journalist – but didn't.

Steadman continued. 'Listen, I just wanted to let you know I was OK. I'm on a payphone here and the beeps have started again. Let's catch up when I'm back in London.'

'Yes. Bye,' said Mackay quickly, but the line had gone dead.

Before Mackay could digest what the journalist had said, Mandy popped her head in the room and caught his eye. 'Inspector Woodhouse's in reception. Shall I send him up?'

'Yes, thank you,' replied Mackay, still dazed by Steadman's call. Was Craven telling the truth after all? The deaths in Northumberland, Peter Vassallo, Bridger, Platt…all accidents? His own attackers nothing more than desperate drug addicts looking for a fix, nothing to do with Craven – the only link between them and Craven being in Mackay's fevered imagination. Maybe there was nothing in any of it, but Mackay didn't care. Woodhouse's investigation would throw up enough mud to do some damage, and that was all that mattered.

The phone rang through from Bridger's office into the boardroom. Mandy was not at her desk, so Mackay dialled *3 and picked it up.

'Jonathan Bridger?' said the voice.

'Yes,' replied Mackay without thinking.

'My name is Richard Garcia of the Gibraltar and West Mediterranean Bank. Can I ask you a few security questions?'

'Of course,' replied Mackay firmly. He quickly opened the file in front of him and turned to the 'statutory books' section where the details of the company's directors were kept.

'Can you give me your date of birth please?' asked Garcia.

Mackay quietly turned a page. '7th May 1945'.

Garcia paused. 'And your address?'

Mackay turned back to the previous page and found the information. 'Little Mill, East Chirnside, Kelso, Roxburghshire.'

Now for the password, thought Mackay. He thought back again to the social conversation he'd had with Bridger shortly after he'd taken over the audit from Platt. Bridger had talked about his family and his children, Steven and Yvette. Mackay scribbled Steven and Yvette on the post-it in front of him. He couldn't remember the name of Bridger's wife – was it Victoria?

'Can you give me the third letter of your password please?'

If it's not Bridger's wife that's easy, thought Mackay. 'E.'

'And the fourth letter?' continued Garcia.

'V' or 'T', thought Mackay. 'V,' he said softly.

'Can you repeat that please?' asked Garcia. Mackay panicked – has he misheard me or is it the wrong letter? He decided to switch children.

'T.'

'Can you repeat that please, Mr Bridger?'

'T for tango,' gambled Mackay.

There was a long pause, then the banker continued. 'And finally the last letter?'

'E for echo.'

'Thank you, Mr Bridger. That's us through the security checks. Mr Bridger, it's about your account, which you recently asked us to close.'

'Yes,' replied Mackay. He was feeling nervous, fraudulent and excited.

'Well, following your instructions we remitted the £7 million into the account you gave us at the Southern and London Bank.'

'That's right,' said Mackay. He briefly thought of his conversation with Alex Williams – the bank's CEO was cleaning up the mess quickly.

'Unfortunately, the interest that was due on the account hadn't been credited at the time of the transfer, Mr Bridger. I do apologise.'

'I see,' said Mackay, in a much firmer tone, 'and how much is the interest?'

'£507,142.'

Garcia waited for 'Bridger's' response. Garcia had been personally responsible for the error and been told to rectify it at no extra cost to the bank. This had been Garcia's third mistake that year. He prayed that 'Mr Bridger' wouldn't make a fuss and the matter could be resolved quickly and amicably. Fortunately for Garcia, 'Mr Bridger' had no intention of making a fuss.

'Mr Bridger, I'm calling to confirm that you wish us to remit this interest of £507,142 to the same account at the Southern and London Bank that the principal went to.'

Mackay glanced at his briefcase and saw the welcome pack he'd received from the Gibraltar and West Mediterranean Bank from John Benady, his uncle's Gibraltarian solicitor. Mackay put down the phone, pulled the documents from his briefcase and spread them across the desk. He quickly found the statements showing his account details.

'Are you still there, Mr Bridger?' asked Garcia.

'Yes, I'm still here. I would like you to transfer the funds to the following account in your own branch. The account is in the name of Thomas J. Mackay and the number is 0083216.'

Garcia repeated the details and Mackay reconfirmed them. A flicker of suspicion had crossed the banker's mind but this had been suppressed. Not only would there be no complaint, but a large sum would remain with the bank.

'Thank you for your time, Mr Bridger. Your account is now closed. I already sent out confirmation of this to you last week, so I see no need to bother you with any further paperwork, unless you want it?'

'No, that won't be necessary,' said Mackay, fearful that a fresh statement outlining this recent transfer would find its way to Group internal audit, and then the police.

'Well, thank you for your business, Mr Bridger, and I wish you good day.'

'Goodbye,' said Mackay weakly. 'Garcia, wait!'

Mackay glanced through the windows across the room to the lift. The doors opened and he saw Inspector Woodhouse and Sergeant Thorpe. Mackay gently removed the post-its from the file and took out the fax from Avon and General showing the £7 million rebate.

'Are you still there, Mr Bridger?' asked Garcia.

Mackay glanced at the waste paper bin, then the fax – it would take less than a second to rip it up, then who would know?

There was frustration in Garcia's voice. 'I'm sorry, Mr Bridger, but I can't hold any longer.'

Mackay had made up his mind. 'Sorry to keep you waiting, Mr Garcia. I...'

A minute later, Mackay closed the file and stood up as the policemen entered the boardroom.

'Good morning, Inspector.'

Printed in Great Britain
by Amazon

40459469R00108